The Trapper

Other publications by Michael Glover

Poetry:

Measured Lives (1994)
Impossible Horizons (1995)
A Small Modicum of Folly (1997)
The Bead-Eyed Man (1999)
Amidst All This Debris (2001)
For the Sheer Hell of Living (2008)
Only So Much (2011)
Hypothetical May Morning (2018)
Messages to Federico (2018)
What You Do With Days (2019)
One Season in Hell (2020)

Others:

Headlong into Pennilessness (2011)
Great Works: Encounters with Art (2016)
Playing Out in the Wireless Days (2017)
111 Places in Sheffield You Should Not Miss (2017)
Late Days (2018)
Neo Rauch (2019)
The Book of Extremities (2019)
Thrust (2019)
John Ruskin: an idiosyncratic dictionary (2019)
Rose Wylie (2020)
Whose? (2020)

As editor or contributor:

Memories of Duveen Brothers (1976)
Goin' down, down, down: Matthew Ronay (2006)
Between Eagles and Pioneers: Georg Baselitz (2011)
Robert Therrien (2016)
Monique Frydman (2017)

The Trapper they called him,
that man Joseph Tredinnick,
late of Porthcothan Bay, Cornwall
– and, my god,
what an inhospitable spot that was in those days!

Why'd they call him that though?
That's an easy one to answer.
On account of his being a **rabbit trapper** by trade
all his free life.

Why else though?
Why? Well, because he kept them **trapped**
in that dirty old caravan of his, all those little ones…

And what of the wife?
Oh, he kept her **trapped** there too,
that poor, long-suffering wife of his…

But didn't he kill her?
Not so much killed as freed, that's what they say,
those that knew her.
She was well out of it, that poor soul, they said…

And what of Tom Trethewy of Newlyn East?
Didn't Tredinnick make away with him too?
Poor, simple soul that he was, Tom Trethewy.
I bet he wished he'd never been made
keeper of the key to that chapel…

And how did God get involved in all of this?
God? Well, they do say it was God that drove him to it.
They do say it was God – or, at least,
his own queer notions of God – that was the real **trapper**.
Tredinnick was just one of God's poor **trapped** creatures.
But I wouldn't know about any of that…

The Trapper

Michael Glover

To Ruth

On Porthcothan Beach

I will admit that Deg's fears looked fresh-faced enough; nor would this vigorous child of my loins have denied it to himself. A ruddy countenance is often as not free of deception, they do say. I had him happily suspended by the legs over that unfathomable rock pool. His cheeks were flushed as the rising sun, and he was blowing out air as fast as if to say: heed me as I hang here, desperately suspended between life and death. I chomped at the fat of his left buttock, and he arched up gracefully over the water – a remarkable feat for one not blessed with the shape of a swan. Would I – or would I not – let him die? It is all one to me, I smiled reasonably. God will not deny me his grace, whatever the issue.

Indifferent or not to my prize, I let it slip through my fingers with a heart-felt sigh. Fate speaks through my hands. Head buffets stone, and I catch my waving reflection, arms still held aloft. Such simple, irregular acts give the evening of a Spring day its vital edge. The gift of my dear Delphine has now passed from me. So be it. The truth whispers; water babbles.

I trust not, for my holy health's sake.

And now we are five – or is it four? Delphine will not trouble to count them from her bed as I coax them up to her – that last, tender household ritual before the light fails me. Her palsied arm rises in weary salutation – or do I imagine it? She is asleep again before we have retraced our steps to the flimsy door. We are at our most cheerful when we breathe the fresh air together – despite storm, sea-wind or the sand which whips off the dunes. Freedom from want – that which my Deg, formerly mine now His, understands most perfectly. I have begun to pool my resources.

We met often – our faces especially – across the chess board which I fashioned for his seventh birthday, and which young Jamie has now buried in the corner of his kennel. He strove hard and often – his young face bright with sweat – to mate me. The youngest, the most dispensable to a father, must suffer if the others are to survive.

And so I have thrown him this sop of a board which he can scarce carry off. It was right of me to stow the pieces, for they are of the best ivory and most to be coveted by the other, bigger ones; the bigger, the more wilful. Sand and wave share with God my complicity – and none other. Do not misunderstand me though. I spread my pleasures as the sand spreads its grains. All are welcome to eat with us, though the space be tight.

Now hear this tale for it is pertinent to all that follows. During those fearful years of myxomatosis, the hardier members of the rabbit clan would drag themselves to the beaches to soothe their pain-wracked bodies in the salt tide. And there they would lie, and twitch, and die. We have a similar dislike of those bloated emmets that invade our beaches at the least glimpse of the tender spring sun. And I have it in mind to drag the body of my dear dead one, daub it in red paint from top to toe, and picture it stranded on the beach here just within reach of the wave's lap. At midnight, of course. And this picture I will send to our *Bugle* paper, together with a baleful tale of the poisonous influences which have invaded the waters hereabouts – three, six, ten miles to the south and another ten, fifteen to the north of our Porthcothan Cove… May God be praised for the upcoming silence of our native shores. Nor will the farmers much trouble me neither, I doubt not.

Lenny whispers into my ear at dawn, and I take her up, frail and brittle that she is, into my cot and comfort her as best I can. Delphine sleeps still beside me, blowing heavily through her lips, and Dorin crawls up and down the space between cot and wall, pushing before him the small bear which was once orange and lost its head. A long, trailing whine issues from his mouth as he labours along on his scrawny knees, back and forth beside us.

As I watch him, Lenny draws my hand down from the head which I have been caressing to her wrist, points – and begs me look. The sores have spread up from her wrist, and she has scratched them until they have bled. Tearing a strip from my cover, I bind up the wrist and haunt her with stories of what will likely become of her if she continues to worry at that poor left wrist with her strong right hand. Thankfully, the right arm is free of sores. Lenny's head disappears beneath the cover when I reach the highest pitch of my haunting tale. She begs me not to continue. She cries out. I yank her head out and slap her smartly – left cheek and right cheek – to restore the good sense to her bleary eyes and trembling head. These children will ever find truth in a story, no matter how foolish it seems to me.

I ask her what she will do with her bright new morning, and she puts a finger to her lips and tries – without replying – to stare me out. I cannot abide such nonsense, and yet I will not chide her a second time so soon.

'Tell me, Lenny, who you will see, and where you will go, and what you will do.'

'Hopscotch…' she mutters twice or thrice before I understand the word. I raise a questioning eyebrow. Now she is ready to oblige me, that little miss caprice.

She jumps out of the cot and begins a small, graceful dance on light feet. First her bandaged arm flies up for hand to touch crown of head, and then the other does likewise. Her feet skip in time to the flailing arms, and the whole flimsy floor bounces along with her. I guess it is one of those endless rounds of dance which the teachers are so perfect at teaching them. I tell her that she must not dance that day or I will beat her. She stands, stone-still, in her fright.

I will wait beyond the railings of the playground out of her – and their – sight, I tell her. And I will listen for her tread, which I can separate out from all the rest with no trouble at all. If she so much as raises a foot or opens her mouth, the dogs will have her supper. And not today's only, I add to press my authority on her.

She slips out of that caravan door without a single word more, and I smile to myself that I have checked her.

If Delphine were awake, she would understand. Dearest Delphine! I lean across to see how well she knows me today. Today we will perhaps begin our lives anew. I ease back the skin of her eyelid and regard her pupil, which stares blankly back at me. I close the eye again – and likewise my own in silent prayer for the afflicted. Having pulled down the strap of her gown, I breathe on her cold nipple and knead it between thumb and finger. It is small and firm as a lead pellet. I will sing to her.

Having made her decent again, I fit the handles of the Melodeon across my knuckles and pump the familiar chords in and out, mouthing the words as I go. I do this to encourage her to join me. She will not sing if I do not sing also. Dorin rises to the sound of the music and begins to clap. I warn him with my eyes not to speak or sing for fear of discouraging his mother. He falls to his knees again and disappears quickly into a corner.

I shall sing in her stead to cheer myself. I rise from the bed and work myself up by stamping as I sing and play. Their several faces are pressed against the fogged window in wonderment. The fine rain has plastered their hair to their heads, and yet they still manage to grin at me and point. I fling away the Melodeon with an almighty clatter and make a violent motion with my arm which tells them to be gone – or else. I throw open the door of the caravan and breathe in several gouts of fresh misty air.

Lenny is crouched there at the bottom of the steps, all wrapped in on herself and motionless. Her head is tucked into her folded arms. I nudge her gently with my foot, causing her to rock for a moment. Our Madge comes creeping from around the corner of the caravan, and whispers words which I do not easily catch into her sister's ear. They scuttle off together, twittering noisily.

I frown at their backs before raising my head to the sky. It will surely be worse before it is better, I tell myself, and fold my arms about my person for the comfort it will impart. I count the others as they idle past in front of me – one and then another… Of the number we have made, three boys and two girls. Until yesterday, I remind myself, boy outnumbered girl by one. It is no longer so. By the shrug of a shoulder, I indicate that the past is behind me and this new bountiful, beautiful day has begun. We will set it in motion by searching the rock crevices for the bits and pieces of clothing whose loss those filthy emmets never seem to notice. Even they have their uses, although I would not have them guess it. It is a race apart, and I would not have matters otherwise for I fear the loss of my pride.

Through the railings I see her, that Lenny, in the furthest corner of the playground. I have been as good as my word. I have not lost faith with myself. She is skipping furiously – and yet I never bought her the rope which she asked for. I told her that rope of any kind, coiled and whipping rope, is a dangerous thing, and I will not have her enter into needless dangers. And now she is skipping with such a rope! It requires much labour to clamber on top of the wall which overlooks their playground. It is a thick, old, cob wall, and I will not lose my balance for by mid-morning the wind has fallen. Even the wan tufts of the grasses are not stirring.

Seven or eight of them are joined in a ring around her, whirling in a ring about her, as she jumps to miss the turning rope. She is so distracted by her pleasure that she cannot understand the danger. I cup my hands to my mouth and call her urgently with full voice.

'Stop, Lenny! Lenny, stop! Lenny, listen to the

voice of your very own father!'

Her skipping stops, and they all turn in my direction. The whole playground has ceased its movements, and from between the frozen bodies of the children the Tattler (or Tittle-Tattler as I call her to make the children squeal when we are alone together) walks heavily to confront me, bony hands on wide, bony hips. I shall watch her try to outface me. She uses so many words, this one, and the rude teacherly manner never fails her. Perhaps she thinks that I am one of hers…

But I am not to be removed from the top of my wall, which I call the rock to myself, such is my grim determination. She shouts up, Mister, to come down from that wall, and stop shouting at your daughter, for she is doing you and no one else any harm.

So few of them understand me. I will not be outfaced by this spinster.

'What you do not see, spinster Tattler, is the terrible danger lodged in that rope which she is flicking and whirling about her. I am here to tell her – and you for that matter if you did not learn of such matters in your college–'

Then, all of a sudden, the child drops her rope and starts to run, screaming as she goes, helter-skelter across the playground, weaving in and out before she finds the gate.

I jump from the wall and swivel to watch her running. She is out of the yard and going as fast as her legs will carry her along the lane in the direction of the sea. I will not take chase at my age.

Now there is nothing more to be said. The teacher has been taught that she cannot stand between my wishes and my family. Yet she is shouting at me again – but too afraid to come nearer, I guess. I hear her speak of Deg. She asks after him. I shake my head brusquely and do not trouble myself to reply. That woman is light-headed, I tell myself. Every day she runs away from the goodness of her own nature, and her words will corrupt me if I heed them.

Perhaps they must all stay with me, those children. There is more to be learnt in the company of self and the dunes and the sea than in all the world's hard playgrounds. I toss a rock lightly into the playground and it misses her by feet. She jumps up and down, screaming, and promising that without a doubt she will report me for assaulting a woman.

'Where is that woman?' I ask, and laugh at her joke. She does not understand why I laugh at her words. She has picked up the stone easily with two hands and she is staring at it, disbelieving, the fool. Yes, it was my meaning, and it is stone through and through without a doubt. The children clamour at her skirts and gawp and point at my stone. It is more famous than I shall ever be. Now she carries it towards the house of the caretaker, which means, I suppose, that I shall hear of it again.

I am determined now that they shall not return

here. Some of those mites have pressed their faces against the railings – one pops right through to his surprise – and they jeer at me, for they do not take me seriously. The Tattler has shouted to them that my wits have gone. They are afraid of me. But before they run away they must frighten themselves with a better view of me.

I run towards them, honking like that dear goose which we ate more than a year ago, and which I have ever regretted eating for its behaviour entertained me. I flap my arms and make great clouds of dust by scuffing up the dusty verge with my feet. I flap and honk and squawk, and they skitter and scatter away, coughing and crying. Sometimes I think that these children learn their bad habits of underestimating me from their adults and teachers. They would know otherwise that I am their fast friend, just as my Madge and my Dorin and my Jamie and my Lenny and my Deg know it. If they belonged to the kingdom of my family, they would not be surprised by my harmless tricks.

The Tittle-Tattler is another matter altogether. I hear it said that she was born upside down and wrong way round. Which must be why she has never wed. She is evidently a teacher of warped and poisoned notions, and she will not approach my brood again.

As I wander homeward, I peer into the hedgerows, for I expect to find Lenny there. I will send the others out for her before I give the dog her supper of today and tomorrow. She must see that she has been a contrary girl. To hear of the loss of her supper from a sister or a brother is not sufficient for her good, nor to see the dog trailing a remnant of it to its kennel. She is fly enough to yank it from its teeth to be revenged upon me, that one. It is not a family business only. God knows and judges my deeds. He must be satisfied that I have done right by her.

When we are at table, they sit and stare as if I have done them some wrong. Something in their eyes asks me why Deg and Lenny are not at their places on the bench. I will let them bide their time before explaining what has become of him. They are too inquisitive; they must learn to wait on my favour.

Madge grabs at a whole handful of bread and goes to drop it into her chicken broth. I tell her to wait until I have counted the pieces. They watch me count. I do it slowly, deliberately, picking up each one separately and putting it aside again. It is three each, and, grudgingly, Madge takes her share without looking at me. She scrabbles at the crumb flecks on the empty plate. I know that she is cursing me under her breath. Had she taken what she had first allotted to herself, she would have had five – albeit two of those were smaller than the rest. Nevertheless, the bigger must not lord it over the smaller and weaker. She has much to learn yet, and I am determined that she shall not go about her wilful business without a teacher to correct her.

I clear my throat and tap the table with the wooden spoon which has stirred and served the broth. All their eyes are upon me now, although some have the dripping spoons part way to their mouths. It is a quiet circle of obedient eyes. Without raising my voice, I tell them that school is over, and henceforth all their learning will be from my hands. They stare, their mouths agape. I tell them that if a teacher or an inspector comes to tell them that they should be in school, and that I am wrong to keep them from their lessons, they should pay no heed. They should go about their business and not speak to the person. If he – or more probably some meddlesome she – asks them again why they have not attended, they must point the way to the caravan and I will speak with these official people.

The younger ones scramble down from the bench and are shouting and laughing that it is all over for them, the schooling; that life is a playtime and nothing more as far as their small eyes will let them see.

Dorin says nothing as usual. He sets to crawling again, and it is as much as I had expected of him. His brain is dark. I deal with him as best I can. Madge it is who is not happy. She is hunched over her broth, and its steam is rising up into her face, making the cheeks redden and shine with sweat. Her spoon is tapping the side of her bowl; and she is breathing heavily. This Madge is the eldest now, somewhere between the ages of ten and twelve, I believe. She likes her school, and she has not shown me her books since as long as I can remember for she guesses that the school and I are not friendly.

She opens her mouth after several long minutes are past and tells me that she must go there. She *must* go. What will she do if she cannot go? she asks me with those anxious eyes which are shifting about the table top as she speaks. I tell her that I will teach her all that she will need to live her life to the full and brimming over, and, into the bargain, make it a happy one. I will even take her to Bodmin and walk her past the lighted windows of the fancy shops at Christmas if this is what she wants especially. I know at least that it is a part of what she wants especially.

Suddenly, she sobs aloud the name of her mother, and I can think of no way to reply to her — except to grip her face until she is calm again.

I rise up from the bench and make to touch her. She will not let me near her, dodging past me to the bed where Delphine is lying in her everlasting beauty sleep. She yanks back the cover and climbs in beside her. She attaches herself to her mother, wrapping legs around legs and pushing arm through arm. I will not try to release her for I see that she clings like a limpet as she shakes and cries.

I pat her back with my hand, and the best I can do is to whistle a tune which I know to be a favourite of hers from many years ago. It seems that she cannot – or will not – hear me. I have pushed myself to the limit to do my best for her. Again I have pushed myself to the limit. These words turn in my head, doing their level best to soothe me.

And then I see the face of Lenny in the doorway. It is white as baking powder. She is looking past me at her sister. I cannot make my anger rise enough to chide her for running away from me in that playground. I know in my heart that it is she who is best to comfort Madge.

I rise to my feet and make way for her. I make a grimace which is all I can manage by way of greeting, and point to Madge. Having fulfilled my obligations, I snatch my cap from its peg and whistle the dog for its walk. I shall take a little thinking time and inspect the bins which they have scattered about the dunes for what of value may be found there.

It will delight them all if I return with a close-wrapped parcel of fresh-ish cake.

This dog, I think, is a freak for it has never obeyed me, no matter if I shout myself hoarse, beat it with sticks, or speak to it as if it were a normal member of the dog kingdom. It was said by she who sold it to me to be close to a sheepdog, but I see little resemblance. I have seen no way to putting a stop to its infernal scratching – which is ever impeding its progress. It is a slouching, careless dog that has never walked in a straight line nor taken a path to a gate without stopping to wait or turn or circle until I am worked up by my shouting into such a frenzy that I can abide it no more as a companion. I hurry on and have nothing more to do with it. At which point, it lollops up, jumping at my face for praise or games. Games, I ask you! I whip it up, and it yelps enough as if to say it cannot believe that I am capable of such things. It goes to lick and nuzzle my hand after I have whipped it as if to declare that it is still my greatest friend, no matter what strange fit may have led me to think so badly of it. Patience, patience, mister, I must say to myself in the presence of that dog.

Why must I forever rein myself in?

Now it snatches at my leg as I tumble on my awkward feet down the steps of the caravan. I toss a curse or two in its direction as I slide and plunge across the sand. We idle amongst the dunes, each inquisitive to know what the other is seeking. Suddenly, I hear a voice behind me and I stop until she catches us. Once she is abreast, I begin the stiffer climb up the cliff path. She runs and walks beside me, slowing me at every end and turn with her questions and her explanations.

I do not like this girl Madge. I have never liked her even if she has been her mother's favourite and therefore the most favoured of the household. She is stubborn in her asking of the same questions about her mother, and I am stubborn in my refusal to give her the replies which will please her. The dog is worrying at her ankles as she stumbles along. This incenses her, it seems, yet she will not be dissuaded.

'I must know this, father. I must know what the man said to you and what you said to him. At what hour of the day did he come to see her and how long was he with her?'

'It was a little before you came back from your schooling. Did you not hear his blue van coughing along the school road?' She regards me with suspicion. She says that she neither heard nor saw that van. And, what is more, she adds in defiance, she wonders whether the healer ever came at all if I cannot tell her what he said to me about her poorly mother.

I whirl around to face her. My hands are trembling. They nearly rise to strike. And then I think better of it for I have decided to be sweetly reasonable with them all or they may return to that school and the influence of the Tattler, which would be the worst outcome possible for this family. I will quell her with my words alone.

'You are a stupid, stupid girl,' I say, grabbing her right wrist and wagging my finger in her face as I speak my straight words to her. 'Just because I do not tell you what this man from Truro has said to me…'

'So he came from down Truro way, then…'

Here is an honest opening for me. I take it.

'Your mother is sick, Madge, and I must have the best person for her sickness even if it means going as far as Truro to find this healer.'

She is silent. I lower my voice so that she will know that I have decided of my own free will to confide in her and be proud of it.

'You are too young by far, Madge, to know what God will do for your mother. He has a plan for her – just as he has one for you and me – and even this dog…'

She looks down at the creature in wonderment. It is scratching at its rear end with a furious dedication. When it sees her staring, it begins to wag its tail and pant and shivery-shake.

'Enough of the dog, Madge, or it will excite itself too much for its own good.'

Now I kneel and draw her towards me. I place the palm of my hand across her back to try to steady her. Her taut, skinny body is trembling.

'Madge, your father is a good man who follows God and knows how serious a business it is to let Him shape our lives.' I run my fingers through her hair. I caress with my fingers her small, damp skull. 'He has shaped this head of yours, Madge. He has made it in just the way he wanted, and when He is ready, you will go back to Him. For we are here only for as long as He wants us to be.'

Her lip begins to curl. She whimpers. I set my arm about her shoulders.

'It is a cold world, Madge, and without your father, you will not find your way. You must not question me so about your mother. When the time comes to tell you more, I will make it known to you. As for today…' I gaze up into the sky. A kestrel is making its lazy wheel above us. '…it is enough to say that Mr Henderson of Truro has been to see her and has examined the soles of her feet. He has studied her feet painstakingly. He has taken them in his hands and kneaded them. He has pushed his long fingers between the toes and he has examined the skin between those toes…' I sigh just to think of it. 'As far as he has examined – and he must continue his work next time for he has only completed the beginning of his tasks – he tells me that they are without blemish. The bones are absolutely perfect, and the skin is smooth and yellow, without corn or carbuncle. He has assured himself that these parts of her are whole. He has washed them, prayed over them, and kissed them. That is the whole of what he did for her yesterday, and I am well satisfied with his work.'

'But what does this all mean, father?' she asks. Her eyes are still shining with tears of uncertainty and apprehension. Her curiosity reaches out too childish far for her own good.

'Madge, it is not for you to ask this question. Your father has not asked Mr Henderson. Nor must you me, I say. Presently, presently, we shall see how it all adds up.'

That dog could wait no longer for its attention.

It was pushing up at Madge's legs from behind and curling its own about her, as if to say: you have confabulated for far too long, and now it is my turn to be heeded.

I pat her about the head once more before they strike off seaward. They run, the one beside the other, along the sand and my mouth stays firm shut. Let her go back and talk of what I have said to her, and let them make of it what they will. I shall not trouble myself with their thoughts of me. They do what they please. I am after a prize amongst all this refuse. If it overspill their bins, the better for me.

Just the Two Together

When presently it comes on to rain, I shelter beneath an overhang of rock which takes my weight and bulk precisely. I am at sea level again, and they have all gone running for shelter.

Through the rain, which is pressing and driving so hard that it pits the sand and gives the rocks a fierce black sheen which they have not had for many days, I see my young Delphine approaching with her father. Their arms are fondly linked, and they push against each other to make as much of each other's company and as little of the rain as possible. It is clearly a good yarn that he is spinning, for her shoulders are shaking, and I hear her high laugh in spite of the wind and the rain which fill my ears.

I am so apprehensive of this meeting, and yet I know that I must try for both our sakes. When we have met in private, she has told me that next time I see them together, I must try. I must try. Next time, I tell her. And 'next time', I gravely tell myself, wondering whether I am still a truthful man.

And here is this next time. It is walking towards me, and she has seen me. I cannot pretend to myself that she has not seen me. Dragging my coat about my person, and stuffing the unruly clumps of hair beneath my cap, I run out to them. It is a strange, loping run, for I am slipping and slithering on the sand. He has ceased his gabble to stare at this running rock creature.

I am within a few feet only of him when my legs shoot away from me, and I sprawl like something freshly grounded by the sure eye of a marksman. It is his eye which has brought me down, I lie fearfully to myself, knowing full well that it is my legs that have lost their balance on that treacherous sand.

I dare not look up at him – and yet I must. I tell myself that I must. I hear him breathing, and I see the boot on the end of that skinny leg, clad in a grey flannel trouser with a patched turn-up. It is a long boot with eight or nine holes for the laces, and the laces pass dutifully through each and every hole until they meet in a double bow at the top.

He is a firm man, I tell myself, as Delphine begs me with her eyes, and more than her eyes, to declare myself to him. All of a sudden, and just as I am about to take the pressure of raising myself onto my arms and spread hands, he puts his boot on my shoulder perilously close to the ear. I am fully afraid of him now, and I dare not budge. And yet there is no measure of weight in that boot of his. It is tapping my shoulder lightly as if daring me to speak; or perhaps he is using me to rub a little sand from his toe cap with no other thought in his head…

Now I hear him speaking to Delphine again.

'…and on the postcard that my sister sent us, I had a nigh-on perfect picture of those palms, the very ones which shook about so crazily when it stormed on the first morning of our honeymoon in Torquay. It was like some mad woman that I once saw in the hospital who jammed her hands against her ears and, with her eyes closed tight shut, shook her head with such violence that I thought she could never be normal again after giving her poor brain such a fearful battering. And yet, on the morrow, she offered me a cigarette – which I refused, of course…' Did he laugh?

Most certainly, I heard Delphine sigh. Then she was silent again. Was she looking at me now? I wanted, like that woman of whom he had just now spoken, to shake my head, and to go on shaking it until the words fell from my mouth – any words would have done, even the very least. But they did not ever come. Instead, my teeth began to chatter, and I could only moan to myself quietly that this was not after all the next time.

When I open my eyes again, they have departed who knows where, and I have within my grasp a pinkish razor shell. I see it is ajar, and I sniff at the liquid inside it. No, it is not the rain or the sea water of my imaginings, but blood from my own hand, lately cut in the squeezing of the shell. And, in spite of all that pressure, it is undamaged, this fine beach shell… Just then, an idea is beamed into my heart. It will go to make a necklace for

Lenny. I wash it – and my own hand – in the sea before I continue my searches.

I wonder again as I kneel just a yard or two from the lick and the slap of the shallows whether Delphine is truly lost to me. I smile at the sea when I remember that Mr Henderson will lay his hands on her tomorrow, and that I have safe about my person the certificate of proof that he treated her yesterday. I tap my pocket. Yes, it is quite safe still.

Now I stow newspapers to one side of the bin and the rest to the other. Beneath some shining tin paper, I find a good collection of boiling bones which are highly suitable for the broth pot. And beneath yet more paper, and the roughly torn skin of an orange, I discover the picture of such a one as Delphine.

The young body is pressed against a rock. The eyes are staring out the sun, and the head hair is spread anyhow across the rock – like seaweed. The arms are spread loose about it, and there is within that cove nobody for it to know, and it seems to want nobody and nothing but the sun. I turn it over and run my eyes along the rows of writing. I will ask Lenny to read those writings to us all for her practice, and then we shall all share what the picture means – whether it was singing or crying or saying nothing.

I stretch my arms and yawn now that the rain

has passed. I am a fuller, brighter person. I think that the day is starting, and when I see from the sun's position, hanging so low above the sea, that it is soon to be ending, I laugh out loud to have surprised myself so.

The Lesson

It is the habit of this family to sit around the candle after supper, and at such an hour Lenny will read to us from my father's Bible. I have undone the clasp and returned the key to my pocket; but this time, to their great surprise, I lay the big book aside and draw from my waistcoat pocket that picture on which I laid my hands at the bottom of the bin.

I blow on it, wipe it with a pocket rag, and hold it up to the light. I nod appreciatively. No matter that it is rippled and stained with the damp. Nothing has changed in the picture. Nothing could change. The children are shuffling closer together on the bench, for they know that there is some treat in store for them. Their eyes are wide and questioning behind the candle. Lenny is standing straight and serious beside my elbow. She has been ready and prepared, in heart and mind, to take the great book from my hands and open it at the leather marker for five minutes or more.

I half-turn towards her and whisper: 'Nothing will be the same tonight, Lenny. We have a different reading for you here…' I twirl the picture between the fingers of my upraised hand, and she looks at it in astonishment as it moves. How can tonight be so different from the rest? What could have happened to overturn our regular practice of so many months?

She goes to take the picture from me, and I shift it out of reach of her outstretched arm with a knowing smile.

'Wait your good time, girl. It is your father who gives us our reading matter, and when he is ready to give it, you can be sure that he will do so. Now hold your hand out flat to me.'

I hear Madge whisper to one of the little ones. 'Quiet in this room,' I snap, 'or your mother will have something to say to you all when she wakes.' After a tiny whimper, all is quiet again, and I am well satisfied with their behaviour. Lenny's palm is still stretched out flat. I tap the picture against the back of my hand and, when the time suits me, I place it ever so gently on her palm, picture side up.

'Lenny. I want you to hold up this picture and show them all our mother.' She takes the card from her palm with her other hand and holds it up for them. 'Closer, closer, Lenny, for the candle is not so strong at this hour.'

She moves closer, almost thrusting it into their faces so that they have to shift their bodies back to see what is to be seen. I wonder whether she does this wicked little act to spite me. No, she is not as good as once she was, this one.

'You have all seen the picture of this beautiful woman who is such a one as your mother once was in her youth. There was none quite so beautiful as your mother. Even this one, although I call her your mother, has not the hair or the quick eye which your mother had then.'

That Dorin interrupts me with the words: 'But I thought it *was* a picture of our mother here, father. You said it was. Now you say it is not.'

Shout the boy down, that is the only way. 'So Dorin speaks to us. Dorin the dumb speaks for the first time in many days, and all he can say is that I have misled you. You are a foolish boy, Dorin. You must not expect to find the whole truth in my first words. If you had the intelligence, you would continue to listen and piece together what I am trying to teach you bit by bit. That way, you would arrive at knowledge. Instead, you hang on the first thing and make a fool of yourself. And, worse still, you try to make a fool of your own father in front of all his children. Leave the table. Leave this house.'

He crawls down from the bench reluctantly, holding me with his eyes as he goes, scraping his hands along the table until the very last moment. Then he pushes open the door and sniffs the rain. I see him shudder. I see his bones tighten. He turns back towards me, but I cannot see the look in his eye now for the light of the candle does not stretch to the door. I must be firm with this one or his misbehaviour will lose him forever.

'Go, Dorin.'

With a shudder, he jumps down from the bottom step and is away. Lenny turns to speak to me. I see some words of astonishment in her frightened eyes.

'Let your words bide their time, Lenny,' I say, and she draws the picture to her, staring and staring. 'As I said to you before Dorin interrupted us all, this one here—' I tap the postcard in Lenny's hard '—is such a one as your dear mother. And tonight we shall hear from the mouth of Lenny what she has said to her father. Show them the back of that picture, Lenny.'

Lenny turns the picture around and holds it up for them again. She moves it in front of their eyes, obediently keeping her distance this time. Perhaps she is not amongst the worst of them after all, this one. I squeeze her arm gently.

'Enough of your showing, Lenny. Now read what she has to tell us all.' Lenny clears her throat and squints down at the writing.

'*Dear Gerald*,' she begins, too quietly for my liking.

'Speak up, Lenny, or we will not hear the message plain enough. Make your best effort, Lenny.'

'*Dear Gerald*,' she begins again, more loudly and firmly this time. Our interest quickens. Every eye is upon her. I knit my fingertips over the table and watch and listen…

I suppose that I will have to fetch him back later for he is good at losing his way amongst the rocks and cliff paths. Nor will I want him to wander near to the rock pool for fear of what he may see there. I would send that Madge to fetch him, but she is a strayer also and too much of a thinker and a talker for her own good. No, I am my best man for the job.

When I look up, I know that too much deep thinking has made me lose many of the words of that woman. '…*and that we are apart from each other now,*' Lenny is saying. She pauses and brings the picture nearer to her face. She screws up her eyes — as if to say that she cannot understand what is in front of her.

'Try a little harder, Lenny, or I will have to give it to Madge.' Perhaps my words will encourage her to push herself for me. Now she begins again:

'*My father says that I must not write to you, but I am disobeying his wishes. Do not tell on me. If you do, you cannot love me. When I come home again, I will make every effort to see you, no matter that he may find out and beat me.*'

I snatch the picture from her hands. These are not fit words for children's ears.

'That is enough for one night, Lenny. We have all heard her, and now it is time to sleep.'

Madge, that Madge, pipes up from the bench.

'But can we not know what happens to her, father? Will she be allowed to see him when she comes home?'

'I tell you that is enough for one night, Madge. There will be no clear answer to your question here. It is not right for a daughter to go against the wishes of her father. Now I ask you to be silent all and prepare yourselves for sleep.'

I return the picture to my pocket and draw Lenny towards me. I force her down onto my knee, and I turn her head towards me. She looks at me coldly, but I ignore it.

'Lenny, I must know where Dorin goes when he is out on his own. You must tell me which are his tracks and his hidey holes, for if he does not return within the hour, I must follow him and bring him back.'

'I will go to fetch him, father. I know where he will be.'

'That is not what I said to you, Lenny. It does not surprise me at all that you would know his secret places. You are as slippery as he. When you defied me this morning, I did not know where to find you. You are a bad girl, and if you had not read her words so well, you would have been punished. If you do not tell me his secrets, the two of you will be the worse for it.'

Lenny is biting at her lip now. Her eyes are sliding sideways.

'The teacher is coming with the man tomorrow, father. She says that you cannot keep us from school.'

'What do you mean: keep you from school?' I shake her to drive some reason into her body. She lets herself be shaken about like a puppet. She closes her eyes. It is as if she has slammed a door on me and my words.

'Listen to me, Lenny. I am your father and you will obey me. You will all obey me. Even Madge is not above me, though she may think she is. You will have all the learning you need from my mouth. These teachers are full of nonsense and they would destroy my family. I shall not have it. Who is this man that you say she is bringing to me on the morrow?'

She opens one eye. It is almost as though she has been mocking me with her obstinate silence.

'It is the inspector from Bodmin, father.'

'From Bodmin? All the way from Bodmin to see me?' I whistle under my breath. 'No matter, Lenny, where he be from. I shall not speak to him – and you shall not return to your school until I am fit and ready…'

She slips off my knee, and before I can ask her more about Dorin and his hidey places, she has disappeared beneath the blanket where they sleep. I see Madge rise up and go to enclose Lenny's shoulder with her protecting arm, and Lenny push her face into Madge's neck. Her head is shaking, and Madge is patting it and rubbing her back and murmuring something or other beyond my hearing.

It will do me no good to pay them any heed. I rise from my seat to test the brightness of the moon, and I see that things could be worse. Although it be a crescent moon, it is a clear night without mist, and the rain has ceased to fall. It could be poorer weather for following in Dorin's footsteps. I am stooping beside the door, fumbling for my outside boots, when Madge surprises me with her words.

'What are you doing now, father? Why are you leaving us?'

'I am out to find that Dorin and bring him back to his bed. The boy must sleep in his bed tonight or he may slip off in the morning and never be found again.'

'Can I come with you, father?' She talks earnestly to me and I know that I must let her.

'Come then, girl. Pull on those boots of your own and some clothes or we shall both catch the death.'

I feel for the knob of the door and let us out as quietly as my stiff legs will allow. Her teeth are chattering so that I tell her to take my arm. She points with her free hand across the dunes towards the beach, and it is there that we go.

We have walked for minutes together without saying a word to each other when suddenly she stops and cries out.

'He is hereabouts, father. I can hear the boy. It is his rock cave yonder.'

She points towards an overhang of rock a little way up the cliff side. We beat our way up and through a pile of the most obstinate gorse to reach the spot. I am heaving so from this climbing that I am hard pressed to hear the next words she speaks to me.

'I will go to see him, father. You must wait for me here.'

I fear that she has some trick up her sleeve. I catch at her arm as she turns to walk away from me into the darkness.

'I do not want you to be a silly girl, our Madge.' She nods without saying a word and tries to pull away again. I hold her fast as a limpet.

'Did you speak to your mother today when I was out with that dog?'

'Yes, I spoke to her, father – very many words I said to her about poor Dorin and the caravan and the school and the coming summer. I told her about all these things. I lay beside her and whispered them all into her ear.'

'And what did you say about me, Madge? Did you speak to her about your old father at all?'

'Yes, I asked her where you had put our Deg for I have been missing him and you will not tell me where he is gone to.'

'Why do you think I have something to do with his going, Madge?'

'I don't know why I think it, father. But you did not like him, and you would have driven him away from us.'

I cuff her around the face. Her hand flies up to nurse where I have hit her. She tries to back away from me. I still hold her fast.

'He was a noisy boy and always running about and causing trouble. He did not want to stay with us – any of us. He will have gone off to find work of his own down Camborne way. That boy has always said that he would be off and away when he was ready.

'But he has not gone to find work, father.'

This was the voice of a vixen. 'Why do you still say such things, Madge?'

'Because he has not taken his clothes, father. They are heaped up in his corner still. He would not go without his clothes.' I scoffed at that.

'That boy would run from me without a stitch on his back. What good are clothes to Deg, those old clothes of his? He will make his money and buy new and then you will see him again.' She did not reply this time. I lowered my voice.

'And what did she say to all these questions, your mother?'

'That was the only question, father. I was telling her all those things because she would want to know them. She wants to know everything about us, our mother.'

'And what did she say then about all those things you told her?'

'She said nothing, father. She did not even part her lips. She was just breathing quietly and listening to the words I had to give her. But that does not worry me, father. I do not expect her to ask me things. I know at least she has remembered and will not forget again.'

I exchanged a single, barren glance with the moon.

'Sometimes, Madge, you make me so angry with your insolence. Here am I, your father, who speaks to you and listens to every word you have to say no matter how stupid or childish. I am here to be spoken to, and yet you tell me nothing. Absolutely nothing. Yet shy Delphine, who is sick and will not speak back to you, she – she – hears everything.'

'She can speak, father, she can. It is just that she did not choose to tell me what she thinks. But I know that she listens and understands.'

'How do you know, then? Are you so clever that you understand the words of a voice which does not speak? Sounds that are never heard by human ear? You must be more stupid than I could ever imagine, Madge, to say you hear her.'

'I hear her breathing, father, and it is quiet and even. Her chest goes up and down gently, ever so gently, up and down. I put my hand above it, and it rises to meet my palm and falls away again. It is calm, that movement, and it tells me: do not worry. I am coming back to you. Soon I shall be with you.'

'So when will she be with you then? Is it August or September? Or on your birthday perhaps?'

She began to cry and I let her go. She curled up on the damp ground and shook and whimpered.

'You must not lie on that wet ground, Madge. It is no good imagining these things to yourself. It is all an illusion. You will make yourself sick with these words of yours. All the family will get sick, and then where shall we be? She will not be better until Mr Henderson makes her better, and he is coming again tomorrow. He is continuing his good work tomorrow.'

'That Mr Henderson will not help her, father. What will he do to her? What is the good of giving him the money, father?'

What vomit was this issuing from her mouth?

'You are hysterical, Madge. He is a man of God, a healer that everyone hereabouts trusts. We must put our faith in him.'

I heard a rustle in the gorse behind her, which stopped me speaking at that instant. Someone was tittering. Someone was mocking my words… I bellowed and struck out with my stick, but thankfully I missed him; thankfully he was crawling towards Madge and I missed him.

He climbed into her arms, which opened up especially for him. I let them lie there for a good few minutes; but soon it was coming on to rain again, and I prodded them with my stick and bade them make haste.

It was difficult going for I had to carry him on my back. Madge would walk in front of me to test the footings. She feared that I would drop and hurt him, I guess. I grasped her shoulder, and let her lead me like a blind man with its guide. He clung so tight that I was nigh on throttled. I spoke sharply to him once or twice, begging him to loosen his grip; but when I slipped again, he would cling all the tighter, the helpless creature.

The Healer

I watched that small blue van of his come snaking down the lane between the hedgerows. He flung wide the door and heaved his great bulk from the driver's seat, pulling his cloak about him again as soon as he was upright. He said little to me, but his eyes made up for what his mouth did not say.

I had driven them out of his sight for fear that they would disturb his work, but I caught Madge's head around the corner of the wall. With my hand, I made as if to swat her away like some pesky fly, and, sure enough, the head disappeared. He took my outstretched hand and nodded a quick nod as if to say we should not waste God's precious time in this way. I ushered him inside.

He entered the door of the caravan sideways – such was his great presence. I busied myself at the gas burner with his bread and his broth while he went to work on her. He would not have me watch, he said, for these things are between a healer and his god; but I listened keenly for the low murmur of his praying words and for the grunts and the groans and the moans as he worked the flesh of Delphine with his fingers.

How long it was that I stood there and stared into his broth I do not know; I seemed to hang suspended in the air in a trance-like state. He held me there and kneaded my flesh too, I felt, with those great, fat fingers of his. When he grunted, I winced and closed my eyes. He bathed me and cleansed me with his prayers…

Suddenly, a hand touched my elbow and I jumped. I turned to see him standing behind me. He was rubbing his large hands together, pulling and twisting and bending his fingers this way and that as if they were not flesh and blood and sinew and bone at all, but best vulcanised rubber all through and through.

'I am ready for that soup now, mister,' he said, without smiling. I dared not catch his eye for fear that he would extract some terrible confession from me. The hands which cupped his brimming bowl trembled as I carried it from the burner to the table.

'Here you are, Mr Henderson,' I said quietly. 'I hope it is all to your liking, Mr Henderson, for there is nothing more in the place.'

His mouth tautened at the edges just a little.

'He who offers me his best, no matter how small or unimportant it may seem to him – and to others – to be, offers himself whole as a humble sacrifice to the Almighty God.'

I too managed a painful smile and turned towards the window, not knowing what else to do with my person. There they all were, pressed against the pane, sullying it with their breath. I dropped them one furious glance, and they backed off to return to their childish pastimes.

'How long has it been like this, mister?' he asked me. I had not thought his voice so deep and so searching, not until this moment.

'It is as long as I can remember, Mr Henderson. One afternoon – it was such a day as this one, broody with cloud, but the sun strong and bright enough behind the clouds to make the eyes squint up at the sky… I was returning from the beach to the caravan. I could not have been more than fifty yards from her when I saw her stumble as she climbed these steps up to the caravan. It seems that she hit her head against the door or something as she fell, for it was hanging open…' I tried to see it again, but there was a sea mist before my eyes. '…and she collapsed all in a heap at the bottom of the steps…'

I knew that the words were pouring from my mouth like a stream in full spate, and perhaps he did not want to hear them, but I had to tell him. He wanted me to tell him something, and now that I had started I must continue.

'I slapped her face and shouted into her ears as she lay there, but I could not bring her round. I was so frightened that I threw a bucket of water into her face to bring her round. She just lay there without speaking. But her eyes were open. After I threw the water full into her face, the eyes opened, they suddenly opened, and she blinked as if to say: I am back again, mister. Where the devil have I been…'

'Name not the Evil One in my presence,' he snapped.

'I am sorry, Mr Henderson. I am sorry for that. I am just saying over her words… And then she said: what is the meaning of all this water? Is it a storm? Am I drowning? Am I drowning? And she began to scream so that I feared she was going off her head. I clapped my hands across her mouth and shouted to her to be calm, calm, Delphine. Nothing is the matter. It is only water. My water. She turned to look at me, and she smiled an odd smile as if to say: 'Your water, mister? *Your* water? It is God's water. It is His…'

'And so it was, mister. It was wrong of you to say that to her.'

'But what else could I do to wake her? What could I do? Anyhow, she closed her mouth and turned to stare at the empty bucket which lay on its side beside her. She stared at that bucket, and she has been staring at it ever since – so to speak…'

'You mean to say that she has never closed her eyes or spoken a word since that day?'

'It is true, Mr Henderson. That is God's sole truth.'

'Not even at night when the rest of the world is sleeping?'

'She is still lying with her eyes open. I have stolen upon her with a torch in my hand at all hours of the night, and still those eyes are open. They are always open.'

We both turned to look at her. And indeed, they were open now, staring at the door, which was fast shut. He tapped at the table top with the butt of his spoon. I could see him thinking again all the little things that I had told him. I clenched my hands beneath the table and closed my eyes for I had a mind to think back to other matters.

I was loitering in the passage of her house, waiting for him to tell me if I had the work. I needed it badly. I wanted him to come out of his kitchen and tell me that I had it. Then I could run back with my news, and we would eat together in the evening, all three of us, instead of just sitting and hoping. I was standing half on the threshold and half inside the door, not knowing whether I should be inside or out, for I felt very awkward and tamed beneath that roof of his. Especially in the knowledge that she was with him, as I well knew.

He closed the inner door after him firmly and cleared his throat. I could not guess what he had decided for his face was in shadow. His voice, when it spoke, seemed to echo with a bruised black echo.

'If I offer you this work, you must promise me one thing.' He stepped a little nearer. 'But if you do not promise me what I ask, I cannot give it to you, and your family will suffer. But that is your business, not mine.'

His eyes had a cold and watery blueness, and when I looked into them, they seemed not to be staring back at me. They they were, lodged in his head, absorbing the looks of others, but giving nothing back – like some stagnant, moss-choked pond.

'Let me hear your conditions then, for you know I need this work.'

'You have been troubling Delphine again these past Sundays. You have spoken to her after Chapel, and I will not stand for it. I have not granted you permission to speak to my family. Will you promise me now to keep your distance?'

I shuffled my feet, and pinched my nose with my fingers. I was a proud boy with some belief in myself. Being challenged in this way, I raised my head and met his gaze.

'Some days ago you placed your boot upon my shoulder. I did not speak to you as I lay there. Yet I had promised her that I would do so. I had said that next time I would have the courage. And now I have it. Your cruel words have given me the courage. If you do not give her to me, I will take her – and who will be the more sorry then?'

Before he could catch me or send his dogs after me, I had made my escape. I lay on my back in Trerice's climbing field and laughed out loud to myself beneath the blue sky, for it was a clear summer evening. I drew his face with the toe of my boot in a cow pat and, when it was quite ready and finished, I kicked it, and the shit, great, stinking gobbets of it, flew high into the air.

Such blithe times are rare in this life. I nodded to myself as I contemplated that truth.

Now Mr Henderson was clearly finished. He stood beside the door, buttoning his cloak at the neck and stamping his feet. Even a man of God has a body of clay, I thought to myself as I watched him stamp the feeling back into his feet after so much kneeling and crouching. He took the money I was holding out to him, and made as if to speak. Then he sighed.

'It is no better today, mister. I am concerned about her. The breathing is short and shallow and the limbs clammy. God is telling us something plainly, mister, and we disobey Him at our peril.'

'What is it that God is telling us, Mr Henderson?'

'He is saying that the hospital is where she must go now. God has put it into my mind that I cannot work alone. I do not want to fail her. Let the physician heal her now, he tells me. Henderson, your part is over. She must go from here.'

He glanced around the caravan.

'This place is not good for her, mister. It is too damp and too cold by half. You must give her of your best. She must be taken away from here.'

My eyes filled with tears at those words of his. I could not believe for one minute that he had failed me. I fell to my knees and began to claw at his cloak and moan.

'She cannot, she cannot leave me, Mr Henderson. Where would I be without her?'

He grabbed me fast by the hair and yanked my head up.

'You must be sensible, mister. Do you not understand that she will die if she stays here? She is dying already. Look at her. Look into her face!'

I smoothed her face with my hand, and it was indeed whiter than I had ever seen it. I tweaked the flesh of her cheek, for I was desperate to drive some colour back into it. He slapped my hand and told me to hold off. I let my head fall into my hands and sobbed quietly. He spread his big hand across my head and kneaded my temples.

'I want you to promise me, mister, that tomorrow you will take her to the hospital and let them treat her. She must not stay here more than another night or she will pass away and you will have the greater burden of burying her.'

I let his harsh words wash over me, but I knew he was right. I must get her to Truro. But how? I looked up at him helplessly and shrugged my shoulders.

'Must I carry her all that way? How else can I move her?'

'No, you imbecile. They will fetch her if your doctor says that she must go and it is an urgent life-or-death matter. Who is your doctor?'

'I have no doctor. I am the doctor of this family. There is no sickness in this house.'

'*You*? How can you say these things when this woman is dying?'

'It is nothing to do with my doctoring, this illness. She fell, as I have told you.'

'If you have no doctor then, or if, as you say,

you are the only doctor, I will take her away from you. I will do it.'

I sprang up from my seat.

'No, you must do no such thing. We do have one hereabouts, I remember…' Would he believe me? Would this man of God believe me?

'You say you have a doctor, do you, mister? Well, if that is so, she will be gone then to the hospital by tomorrow. Otherwise, she cannot live another day. Do you understand what I am saying?'

I bowed my head humbly.

'Are your words not plain enough then, Mr Henderson? Trethewy shall see her within the hour. I shall go to him and implore him to look after her. My Delphine is seeking a helping hand…'

I put my hand flat on her cold forehead. He turned to leave.

'So be it. I shall come by tomorrow, by which time she will not be here. Is that not so, mister?'

'That is so, Mr Henderson.' I touched my cap to him, and he shuffled down those steps to his van. I held it with my eye until it vanished behind the hedgerow, and then I sat beside her poor self again and set to thinking how I could best dispose of her.

Taking Up the Burden

Lenny had her finger in the Bible. I let her read some words to settle them. Then we would see how they obeyed me – or otherwise.

She paused in her reading to take a breath, and I put my finger to my lips. She stopped and looked at me, her small eyes a weird blaze of puzzlement.

'Will you wait a moment or two, Lenny, for I must have words with you all concerning these matters.' I watched their eyes attending closely. This was the right way to do it. I felt happy then with my plans.

'This is a miracle that we have been hearing of in the Bible. And it was Jesus who performed it – just as he performs all the miracles in this world about us.'

'Did miracles not happen before Jesus then, father? Did you not once tell us of a burning bush, and ladders stretching up to heaven, and such like other things?'

'Jesus is the only one, Madge. You are interrupting me, and I must not be bothered for I have something important to say to you.'

She fell silent, but I could see that I had not pleased her with my words. So be it.

'This miracle of Jesus of which I speak concerns a dead man who was all wrapped up in his burying clothes. Probably he was already beginning to smell a little…'

I saw them shudder and screw up their mouths at these words. And then, raising my finger, I put some light into my eyes.

'And yet, in spite of this thing, our Jesus came to him and told him to rise up from his bed. How could this happen? How can a dead man come alive again?'

I scanned their faces. They did not know the answer, God's answer. 'It is because Jesus is the Saviour of man, and even the deadest people he can bring back to life. I could tell that Jesus to walk into the cemetery of St Mawgan-in-Pydar, and make all those dead people come alive again. They would step out of their graves, those great-grandfathers and great-grandmothers and all the older ones still, and dust themselves down and come skipping back home again.'

Jamie's lip was curling. Madge pushed his head down onto her stomach and continued to stare at me. I had them now – like four little fishes caught fast in the net.

'None of us knows at all how Jesus can do these things, but we know he can because the Bible tells us so… Now this Lazarus, he told him not just to get up, but to carry his bed away with him. Think of it, children. A dead man who can carry away the bed on which he was lying! And the onlookers – all those Pharisees and Jews, all those beggars and women – they watched him in amazement as he unwound the bandages which had been wound round and round his body...'

'Was he white and naked underneath the bandages, father?' Lenny whispered in my ear.

'Of course not, Lenny. He died in his night-shirt, which they did not take off him. It was the custom.'

I spoke aloud to them again. 'And, having taken off the bandages, unwinding them round and round from head to foot as they gawped in amazement, he picked up his bed, balanced it on his head, and went home again. The crowd was so astonished that they kissed the dead man and hugged him, and the children played with the bandages as if it were a Mayday Festival. And everybody clapped Jesus on the back and shook his hand and congratulated him on having worked another of those famous miracles of his...'

They gasped. They had not thought about it in this depth before. Now they would surely understand what I was trying to say.

'Jesus helps everybody, he is everybody's friend. He is ready to do his miracles any time we ask him.'

Jamie looked up.

'But where is this Jesus, father, to do these things? How can he do them if he is not here?'

'I am coming to that, Jamie. Be patient, boy.'

He lay his head back on Madge's lap, but now his eyes were open, listening.

'Jesus went back to Heaven again to be with his father, God, but... he returned here again. This time he did not come in a body. This time he came like a gently pushing wind that moves across the marram grasses, disturbing them, ruffling the grasses' hair, but not itself to be seen...'

I could see they were puzzled. They did not understand all this deep doctrine of God and his strange habits. 'He is a spirit, my children, and he is always with us, always, moving across the grasses, and making the sun to climb up the sky and sink down again, and the rain to wet us... And he can still do such miracles as he did then. He will make a Lazarus live today – if he has a mind so to do...'

All of a sudden, Dorin looked at the door and pointed and gave a tiny little cry.

'It is nothing, Dorin boy. Do not concern yourself with these little breezes.'

He was not to be made happy by my words, however. He crawled to the furthest corner of the caravan and sat down and watched that gap beneath the door which, from time to time, whistled gently.

Now I must come to it. I had prepared them well enough for the news.

'Tonight in this caravan we have a Lazarus amongst us.' They gasped and shifted nervously, looking hither and thither.

'Where is he then, father? Show us.'

'Let me speak more. Stop your fretting and fidgeting and you will know soon enough what it is I am saying...' I coughed to clear a dry wedge of spittle from my throat. 'This Lazarus of which I speak is your mother, Delphine.' They all turned and stared at that great hump of her in the corner. 'She is very poorly, my children, and Mr Henderson tells me that she will be more poorly still if we do not help her. We must all help your poor mother…'

'What must we do, father? What *can* we do, for we are only children?' Madge asked quietly. Her voice was trembling with apprehension.

'There is one thing you can all do, no matter that you are not fully grown. Of what concern is that to God anyway? He has told the children to come unto him and be his servants.' I looked hard into all their faces, one by one.

'And this time it is no different. We shall all pull together to help her. It is the only way. But we must act quickly for the time is short.'

'What, *what* then, father?' shouted Lenny into my ear, full of her usual impatience.

'I shall tell you, Lenny. Your mother must go from this place tonight.' They gasped again.

'But where will she go to, father?' asked Madge.

'We will take her to that place where Dorin hides away from me when I am angry with him.' They all turned to look at the boy. He had hidden his face in his hands.

'But why must we take her there, father?' persisted that Madge. 'Is not this a better place, a warmer place, for her? Surely to be out in the cold will be bad for our mother. She will not be better at all if we treat her in that way.'

I clothed myself in the utmost solemnity, top to toe.

'It is Mr Henderson who says that she must go there, Madge, and he is a servant of God. It is God who has spoken through him to us about your mother. God says that this place is bad for her. Within these walls, the germs breed and multiply, and her body wastes away. Let her out into the open, into the fresh, pure air that blows in from the sea, and she will come back fresh to us in no time at all. She will be, once again, that mother she was until a little while ago.'

I could see the fear and the mistrust writ large upon their faces – especially that Madge's. She did not believe my words. I had to convince her or the others would not follow. I pointed my finger straight at her.

'Do you not want your mother to live then, Madge? Do you want us to bury her in Pydar churchyard with all the rest of the corpses, all those bodies that illness and disease have shrunk away to nothing?'

She stared back at me, saying nothing. The others started to cry and to moan. I beat my fist upon the table for order.

'Enough of this weeping and moaning. We must put it behind us. It does your mother pitiful little good to be cried over. Do not forget that. We must help her and help her quickly.'

I clapped my hands together and rose up from the bench. 'Let us be about it then. It is a clear night without rain or mist. She will come to no harm to be carried in our arms up to Dorin's cave. Let us be about it!

'Lenny, go and fetch that pile of blankets from the corner. In these we will wind her, the better to protect her from the weather if it should turn before we reach our destination. And, Madge–'

'Yes, father,' she replied, coldly and reluctantly,

'–you must have spirit, girl, and trust in what Mr Henderson tells us, for you know he speaks to us with the voice of God. You are to be the leader of our expedition. You will walk a little way ahead of us, preparing the way. You will be a veritable little John the Baptist, Madge – except that you will bear a torch and not a staff for your – and our – comfort.'

She nodded. I knew then that I had won her over and all would be well.

From my sack I drew a hank of stout rope and cut it into several lengths. They gathered around the body of Delphine and watched me at my labours. Now they had ceased to talk. This dark adventure had taken them over.

I had Lenny cross her mother's hands over her chest, and these hands I bound together lest the arms swing loose beneath the blanket or, worse, slipped their moorings altogether and, falling free, caught against the gorse and brambles, or damaged themselves against a rough wall in passing.

Having secured the arms in this way, I bound the legs together at the ankles. Then I tied an extra loop of rope through the last to carry her by at the feet end. If several took the strain together, they would manage that end all right. I would undertake to bear the weight of the more burdensome part – head and torso – being the strongest.

Having trussed her in this way, I tore off a strip of blanket and, folding it into a compacted wad, stuffed it between her teeth. I had a devilish job prising open her jaws but, thanks be to Him, I managed to jam the wad between the upper and lower set of dentures. Delphine has some pride in her teeth, and were she to snap or crack them, no matter how little, her grief would be boundless and, without a doubt, I would suffer and be branded neglectful. Having wadded the teeth, I wound another strip of bandage around the extremity of her face lest the jaw be inclined to slacken.

Yes, I had to prepare her as best I could for the joltings and the jarrings of that upcoming journey.

It was coming on to eleven o'clock now, and those children were some weary mites, I saw. The boy Dorin had fallen asleep in his corner. Even the fear of the wind's moaning had not held his back straight and awake. Young Jamie lay across Madge's lap, who was sitting beside Lenny on the edge of our bed.

I motioned to Madge to position herself at the bottom of Delphine's body. I was standing at the head. We rocked her a time or two, and as we rocked, Lenny began to push the big blanket beneath her, feeding it in little by little as the rhythm of the rocking swung her away from it. I threw it right around her body, which pinioned the arms to the chest and held the legs tight together.

She is a fully mummified woman now, I thought to myself — except that we did not bandage the head for fear of suffocating that poor wife and mother. Then, with all my God-given strength, I began to roll her over and over in the blanket. Lenny was pushing her little frame against the side of the bed just in case all my heaving and towing about sent the body spinning right off onto the floor.

The Madge had charge of the head at this time. I feared to break Delphine's nose with all this heavy rolling onto the face and over. Madge took charge of that nose as best she could. At the second roll, we had her stuck on her stomach, and it seemed that she would not budge an inch or more. The face was jammed into the bed, and I was fearful of her suffocating.

Then, all of a sudden, she began to cough and spit and cough again. The throat, it seemed — or the pipes that led down from the throat — were suffering some great constriction. That great body, inert for so long, heaved and thrashed and churned. Then it fell silent again, but still breathing with a heavy dragging wheeze for the coming minutes.

And all the time it was coughing and churning, I prayed in a fever to God to rescue her, dead or alive, from all that torment, and give us all peace again. Which he did by and by – thanks be to Him.

The body being fully rolled at last, I produced from my sack the best steel pins of my collection, and pinched those layers of blanket together in five or six places. Now she was a fine, snug bundle and I was proud of this handiwork. Except that Madge was still worrying me about that head of hers, which was sticking out of the end without a covering of any kind.

Then I remembered the balaclava, Deg's balaclava, which, after some rooting, we found tucked away snug at the bottom of his box. Turning to Madge, I said: 'It is a good thing then, Madge, that he did not take the clothes with him, isn't it?'

She grunted some reply, but I saw I had weakened her a little in her obstinacy. Cupping her mother's nose delicately with the left hand, she pulled the balaclava over the crown and down the face, making sure first to knot the hair in a bundle on top of the head. And what hair that had been in her prime!

The eyes had not closed when she pulled that balaclava down the face, for when I examined the covered head, I found a fleck or two of wool in the eyes which I tweaked away, ever so delicately, with my finger ends. I tut-tutted to myself to think of this poor woman who had not the good sense to close her eyes as it passed over. She was in a poor way, this one.

Now all was ready, and it was a matter of rousing those who were sleeping – for I would not let them stay here without a father to see to them. I had Madge deal with them as best she could, for I would have been too harsh and too hasty for their delicate, sleeping forms.

She picked up that Jamie and screwed his ears, whispering as she worked. Then she blew on the lids of his eyes, which made them blink open. There was an unhappy bewilderment in those eyes, which so badly wanted their sleep back. She let him slip from her knees, and had him use his legs, which were at first inclined to buckle. She laughed at him, tapping at those rubbery legs, and at last he began to stamp his feet and shout back at her as if he were a marching soldier who had been freshly roused to do battle.

That Madge knew how to deal with these children, there was no doubt of it, and I rewarded her with a smile, which she seemed not to notice. She pulled a rag from her frock pocket and pushed it back at his pushing face. He blew. She rubbed and wiped. And now he was all done and ready – barring boots and a coat. That fine boy turned from her, marched up to me, and hit a driving kick at my shin bone.

The others too were stirring, and now Madge was testing her torch. First she lodged it under her chin and made a ghostly face to please the stirring mites by frightening them witless. Then she let the beam stray down on to that white face in the balaclava. It is like the thief at night, I thought.

'Madge, you must not waste the juice. It is an old battery in that torch, and we do not want to tramp in the darkness with your poor mother, do we now? Think, girl, before you waste your light.'

She snapped it off straightaway. Instead, she bounced the handle of the torch off her legs, first one and then the other, until I told her again to stop spoiling the precious thing.

I wish I had not smiled at the girl. She is ever working against my wishes. She fell to her knees now and put her ear against the mouth of the balaclava. I saw her nod and nod and then listen. What could she be doing? I was not a little afraid of her in this mood.

'Come now, children. It is time for us all to go and take your mother to that place where she will get better; where her poor flesh can breathe in the best of our fine sea air. But before we go, we must do one thing together. We must pray for her and for the success of our journey. Now come all of you and join hands with me around the bed, and I will speak to God about her.'

They approached the bed warily, and one by

one they slipped to their knees, first glancing up at me to make sure that they had not misunderstood my meaning. They thought it a queer enough thing to be doing. We all joined hands, making a ring around our marriage bed. Each of those quiet, staring faces was on a level with that long, swathed figure which stirred just enough for the eye to catch its motion through layer upon layer of blanket.

'Now close your eyes and make sure your hands are all clasped together, for then God will know how earnest are our prayers for her.

'Our father…,' I began solemnly enough, but I could not prevent the slight quaver in my voice. So much hung on this prayer. What if He would not heed us? I quickly banished this diabolical thought from my head and continued resolutely. '…you know why we will be carrying our dear Delphine's body up the cliff path on this dark night.'

I hesitated. For a moment I was lost for words. Must I not be telling the Almighty what he already knew? Still, I reasoned, He would want to hear it from my mouth. He would want me to testify that I believed in Him and His ways with all my heart.

'It is because Mr Henderson, that healer man from Truro, has instructed us to do this for her. And he is your servant, so it must be true…'

I paused again. I expected to hear warming words of reassurance inside my head, but I simply began to shiver with the cold. Dorin sneezed, and I opened my eyes, the better to frown at him. But his were still shut so tight that he was pulling a most ghastly face. It was all I could do to stop a smile spreading across my own. But He would not have taken it well, I knew.

'We have bound her in bandages as best we could – even as the Lord Jesus was swathed as a babe in the manger. With your guidance and protection, she will come to no harm on the journey which is ahead of us. We know that you are always with us, and that you will make it known to us if we stray from the path… the path of the spirit, that is. Lord, smile on these children too, for they surely need a mother and a mother's voice, and, in spite of doing my very best for them, I cannot hope to be mother and father together…

'Yes, we want her to be well again, Lord, so we plead with you to heal her of this sickness which we do not understand. And, if it is your will, Lord, keep it from raining or blowing too hard upon us because the burden of her is great and we would not wish to let our precious charge slip from our hands and down the cliff side. Keep our steps steady, and show us your heavenly light even if that torch of Madge fails us, which may well happen, given that it is an old one and has not been treated with the respect it has deserved. For which we ask you to forgive us also. Finally, Lord Jesus, thank you again for sending us your servant from Truro, Mr Henderson, and we trust that you will give him a long life and let him be a blessing to many people besides ourselves. In the name of the Father and of the son Jesus, and of the Spirit who moves across these waters… Amen.'

When I opened my eyes, I caught Madge nudging awake Jamie, whose head had slumped against the bed. I showed to each his position around the body, and, heaving the upper part of the body towards the edge of the bed, I took the strain.

I made a motion to Lenny to open the door, which she did in too great a haste, for no sooner had it clattered against the wall of the caravan than it flew to again, helped by the rising wind, with a tremendous bang, making the whole inside to shudder. The second time, she caught it back with the hook against the wall, and all was now ready.

'You hold the feet steady, children, and I will draw the head and chest down onto the floor.'

I was careful to keep my boot under the shoulder blade for fear of breaking the neck by resting it against the floor. Soon it was all managed, and we dragged and slid her so that her legs soon began to project from the door. The children clambered over the body and slipped down the steps to take the weight of the feet and the legs. There being a good four steps up to the caravan, they were able to get a firm purchase on her lower half as it slid out into the night air.

Pushing and heaving to left and right to prevent its jamming the doorway – such was the great bulk of those bandages – we soon had her sliding down the steps and onto the damp ground. I knelt down beside her and pressed my ear to her chest. Thankfully, she seemed no worse for this part of her ordeal. I ran my fingers beneath the layers of blanket and shone the torch upon the steel pins. All was holding firm.

And then there began the carrying to that nook in the cliff which seemed to us all a night without end. So many times we nearly dropped her; and many another, a child would start weeping, and I would shout to them all to stop and lower their burden. They would lie across the swathed body for a little comfort, for it was undoubtedly the softest place that a head could rest on. Some were to the left and some to the right, all arms and upper halves draped across her like flags across a bier. Happily, she continued to breathe.

Our progress was so slow that the sun was breaking over the sea before we came within sight of the end of our drudgery. We fought back gorse and dog rose and many another clinging shrub and bush before Madge pointed ahead to a narrow bank of shadow between two faces of a cliff directly ahead.

And then, all of a sudden, Dorin let go of his corner, making things perilously hard for Lenny who almost let fall the body. It was indeed a treacherous place for such a thing to happen, for we were inching forward along the narrowest coastal path imaginable. The weight was so much the greater for her that she had to spin her body in to snatch the blanket up with both hands. And as she turned in to catch it, her right leg shot out behind her and she nearly pitched herself into the gorse beneath and thence down the cliff face. But as she went to fall, I grabbed at the hem of her frock and all, thanks be to Him, was well again.

Except that the Dorin was still running and squealing ahead of us, and I feared that some early farmer would come running and talk his head off that day to all and sundry about our most peculiar procession. So I shouted to the boy, but within seconds of my raising my voice to him, he had turned into that place where the shadow fell horizontal, and had disappeared altogether.

The Promise of the Cave

It was a narrow entrance to Dorin's nook, and we had to turn her around a rock to glimpse the place at all, which was no higher than my knees as I stood to face it. The small ones scrambled in and out, and now they were laughing and whispering because those bad, dark hours of labour were past and all was a flighty child's adventure again.

I knew I would find it some difficult to get myself in there, and the only hope, I saw, was to be dragged in feet first by those children, with myself pushing and scrabbling as best I could with my fingers.

But first there was Delphine to go in, and I wheeled her body around until the face disappeared beneath the flat rock which overhung the entrance. Then I unwound the ropes from her feet. I saw that all that lugging and carrying had made those ankles raw and the flesh very angry. I kissed them and smoothed them, but they were stone cold still at the extremities, and I guessed that it would be some time before the life returned to them.

Bundling the rope together, I threw it into the children, and instructed them how to thread it beneath the shoulders so they could make a harness with which to pull her backwards while I pushed from the outside. I heard them talking and talking about that harness, and how they would manage to do that work I had set them. If she was listening now – as Madge would say she was – she would be proud of their efforts. At last it was all fixed, we set to work again, and soon the feet had disappeared altogether.

I felt beneath the rock to assure myself that the way was quite clear, and then I too sat down and pushed my legs in front of me and under the rock. No sooner were they tucked snugly beneath that overhang than I felt all these pairs of hands begin to grab at my legs and ankles.

I shouted to them to hold off for a minute. I had a mind to rest on my elbow and smoke a quiet pipe of tobacco before slipping into that diabolical dark again. I looked down upon my odd, legless frame and wondered what it would be like indeed to lose those precious limbs which were always at the ready to carry a man wheresoever he wished – beyond the reach of pain and into new havens of pleasure, if God so willed it. And the gloom descended, for this thinking brought it home to me that my life's companion was not merely legless but quite insensible. And I knew at that time for sure that the Madge had imagined all that close communion between them.

And then I looked again at the strange position of my body and, remembering their pulling, I imagined myself a puppet at the mercy of the one above who drags us whither he so chooses, and, when our time arrives, takes the spiritual part of us to himself and disposes of the rest without more ado – just as He had nearly disposed of poor Lenny down that cliff face. Yes, I saw through that almighty pother of pipe smoke that we quickly come and go, and it is a waste to fret overlong about it.

I knocked the pipe against a stone, lay my weary bones down, and shouted for them to begin.

It was not an unhappy place after all, albeit that the dark was not wholly welcome. When I could see again, I found Dorin in the corner playing with his pile of stones. In the centre of the cave, which perhaps measured some twelve feet from entrance to back and was a rough oval in shape, the rocks rose to a point, and here I could stand straight and beat the worst of the dust off my waistcoat and trousers. I saw when I raised my head that it narrowed to a point of light no larger than a half-crown, and I smiled to see that needle's eye of sky directly above my head.

She lay so peaceful and out of harm's way by the wall that they had for the most part forgotten her. Madge alone still hovered there, and now I saw her pulling at the balaclava.

'Do no such thing, Madge. There is no warmth in this place, and we must continue to protect her as best we may.' She stopped and looked up at me, confusion in her face.

'But how long will she remain here, father? Are we not to take her back again tonight under cover of dark so that we can watch over her and feed her?'

'Mr Henderson said no such thing about her

going back so soon. It is God's will that she is here, and she will remain until he gives us a sign through his servant to move her.'

'But who will look after her, father? Am I to stay and guard her?'

I snorted.

'You, Madge! A young, frail girl such as you! Not in the least. This is man's work, and your father will see to her. She will come to no harm. It is needless for you to fret over her. Trust me and God, Madge. You cannot take the whole burden upon yourself. Your thoughts are too old for your body. You must become as a child again who trusts her father. Do not be too grown for your time.'

But I saw that she was still uneasy and disconsolate. She stared and stared at the ground between her feet without once raising her head or replying to my words. I walked over and knelt down in front of her. I lifted her chin with my finger. She continued to ignore me.

'I will let you play the big girl then, Madge, if that is what you wish. For hours at a time I will not be with you. It is impossible that any man should be in two places at once, Madge...'

'What about Jesus, father?' She was squinnying at me.

'That is different, Madge. God is a miracle worker, as I have already explained to you, and nothing is beyond Him. But I am different...' I cleared the gob of spittle from my throat. 'This being the case, I give you these children to care for and to feed and to comfort when I am away from you. Is that what you would wish, Madge?'

'It is my mother that I wish to comfort, father. She needs me more than those others. Let them care for themselves. Our mother is grievously sick and she cannot lift a finger.'

'You are wrong, Madge. They cannot manage their lives without an older one to guide them. Can Jamie prepare his food? Of course he cannot. You are being silly and you know it. I am the best one to look after your mother, there is no question of it. And I, as your father, instruct you to behave like a proper daughter to me and feed and comfort your brothers and sisters.'

She nodded without replying.

'Now we must go back to the caravan, Madge, for they need their rest and their sustenance. They have been a long time without it. I will explain it all to them, and then we will take them away from here. And I do not want that Dorin returning to his cave. He must not leave your sight. Will you promise me that, Madge?'

She nodded again – but I could not weigh in my mind how much she had heeded what I told her.

'And there is one other very important matter, Madge. If anyone asks you what has become of Delphine, you must not tell them the truth for they would not understand you.'

Now she was alert – and puzzled.

'Why should they not understand, father? Why

can I not tell them?'

'You must say that I have taken her away to some relatives up country to be cared for. Say that she has gone back to Dobwalls. That will satisfy their nosy natures.'

'But why not tell them what has really happened, father?'

'Because Mr Henderson has said we must not. This is God's secret, and none other is to know it. God works in mysterious ways, Madge, and he is accountable to no man. It is Mr Henderson's wish that we tell no one.'

'And shall I send Mr Henderson to you if he calls upon us again?'

This Madge has an awkward way with her words.

'What you must say to him, Madge, is this: I have done as he asked, and he must pray now that his remedy will bring her back to us. Say only those words, Madge. He will understand your meaning. The rest I will tell him face to face when I see him. These are private matters and not to be spoken of lightly.'

'When can I see her again, father? When is she coming back to us?'

'I do not know the answer to either of those questions, Madge. It is good that she should know the rest and the quiet of this place away from all your noise and childish fretting. She will be better all the sooner if we give her the peace that her soul clamours for. This is very important, Madge, and

Mr Henderson never ceased to talk of it when he asked me to bring her here...

'I do not want you to forget that if you try to come here against my wishes, or permit any of the others to stray here without your knowledge, I cannot answer for what God will do, seeing that you will have defied his express wishes. This is God's business, Madge. I am only your father. Do not cross Him for he comes with a sword of vengeance when he is crossed.'

I made a little cutting sign in the air – no more than that. She whimpered all the same.

'Do not be frightened, girl. I have to say these things to you strongly or you may not understand their importance. It is her life that we are saving, and God has told us how to act. Think on what I have said, Madge, and do not cross me. When I come down to you and give my permission, then you can see her. Or perhaps in a very few days, we will descend that path, your father and your mother, arms linked together as we were wont to do before the tragedy struck us. You and all the children must pray for that day, Madge. Pray three or more times a day for that time to come to pass, and He will heed your prayers for He is merciful and great... And now I will come down with you to the caravan to collect what we will need.'

I looked down upon them all. Some were still at their games. Lenny was lying on her stomach, arms folded beneath her face. She was staring out towards that thin sliver of daylight.

'Come now, children.' I clapped my hands to rouse them. 'It is time that you were all back in your home, and your mother needs her peace and quiet. Your noise is too much for her so we must be off and away. Are you not hungry, Dorin? Nor you, Lenny?' I prodded her in the side with the toe of my boot. 'Madge will prepare your porridge. Let us all be off and away then. But before you go, we will offer up a silent prayer to God to make your mother well and bring her back home to us as soon as He is willing. Close your eyes then.'

They did so dutifully, and, having counted up to ten, I spoke again. 'Madge, you scramble out first so that you will be there to meet them and save them from harm.'

One by one they crawled out after her, Dorin being the last to go. It took a little time to coax him from his hidey hole. I imagine that he thought we had set up home there. First of all, he refused to crawl beneath the overhang. He knelt there, stubborn as an old blind mule, and no amount of pushing of his bottom or calling out from the others would persuade him to budge even an inch. I would not push him too hard for fear of grazing his knee caps. Then he began to cry, and his whole body collapsed into a sobbing heap.

This was too much for me. I slapped his legs sharply. He jumped aside to avoid my heavy hand. But there was only one sure way of escape and this he knew well.

'Think of your mother, Dorin. Do not be such

a selfish boy.'

Eventually the promise of pain – and yet more pain – proved too much for him, and he was dragged and pushed, screaming, into the light of day.

I preceded them home. They were so cowed by the smacks I had meted out to that boy that they did not utter a single word the whole of the journey. When we reached the caravan, I bade them all enter with the exception of Madge, and she I drew aside for a little conference.

'Now you do remember what you have promised me, Madge, don't you? I do not want you to break any of those promises which you solemnly made. Can I trust you now, girl?'

'I shall not disobey you, father. You will care for our mother and bring her back to us again when she is well.' Her voice was strangely quiet and lacklustre. All the better for her to be compliant than that rebellious, boisterous little person I had known all too often.

'You are a good girl then, Madge.' I kissed her cheek and drew aside her hair, which she had let fall in a lank curtain over her eyes. 'But first remind me what you must say to Mr Henderson when he visits you.'

'I… I…' she stammered and hesitated, '…must tell him that you have taken her to the place she was supposed to go.'

'Anything more than that, Madge – if he

should just happen to ask you?' I gripped her arm as a small aid to concentration.

'No, nothing more, father. I will just say that these are God's matters, and not to be spoken of except by you and him together.'

'That is better that I could ever have dreamt, our Madge. you are my best girl again...' I loosed my grip and patted her on the back.

'Here, girl, I have a little something for you, a little present, which you must not show to the others. It is a sign of my favour – and God's, of course – because you have remembered everything that I have told you.'

I drew from my trouser pocket the little square piece that I had kept all safely wrapped in my old blue kerchief. I fingered its outline beneath the linen. It was whole still. I smiled inwardly. It was good to give a child such as this a pleasant surprise once in a while. She would think the better of me for it.

She gazed with fascination upon the shape as I unfolded the kerchief. Out you come, my beauty, I said to myself with no small satisfaction that I had thought of such a thing for this occasion. I spread the cloth across my palm, letting it fall away to reveal the prize I had for her: a beautiful little square of best cheese.

I picked it up between thumb and finger and turned it in the air. Her eyes were glued to the thing. I looked into them.

'Open your mouth then, Madge. You would

not want them to find you with such a prize, would you, girl?'

I grinned. She shook her head quickly and opened her mouth dutifully. I popped it in, and although it was a little too large for the cavity, a fine bit of fast and spirited munching soon whittled it away to nothing at all. Having swallowed the last morsel, she pecked me on the cheek and fled into the caravan.

Immolation

I made my way, light of heart, a whistle of contentment beneath my breath. As I beat my way back up that cliff path, a squally rain blew in from the sea, and for the first time since I had settled on the plan, I began to question whether it were God's will or no.

I was soon able to put such thoughts aside. I told myself that it was a common enough trick of the Evil One to sow seeds of doubt in the minds of the faithful, and that the only way of putting paid to such dangerous nonsense was to repeat out loud some of the words which the good Lord had himself taught us. I therefore spoke forth, into the wind and the rain, with a boldness and a pride in my delivery which can only exist in the heart of the true believer when he truly feels the Almighty dwelling within – that still, small voice giving him the strength and the purpose to live his life in the way that the Lord has counselled, and enabling him to set at nought the whispers of the Devil.

Soon my old limbs were protesting mightily at all this scrabbling and scrambling about amongst the rocks; but I had chosen the spot myself, had I not, and they do say that endurance is the better part of valour…

Within the hour, thanks be to God, I was lying

beside her, breathing heavily and urging myself to become accustomed to the downward press of the dark again. When I had calmed myself, and rested a good while to regain my powers, I listened out for her breathing.

It was undeniably faint – but, thanks be to him once again, still perceptible. And, as I listened, it seemed to increase in strength and volume. Yet the sounds which I could now hear were surely not a good omen… The breaths were coming harsh and short – almost as if these, her very last gasps, were anxious to be expelled from that failing body as quickly as the machinery of her poor, tattered lungs would allow it. They were rushing headlong towards her mouth, over which I was now bending. And soon – for that is how it seemed to me just then – that last desperate cubic inch of air would escape into the atmosphere where it would then be free to mingle with its own…

I placed my finger upon her lips, which vibrated violently with the expulsion of each new breath. First they seemed to swell and blow apart a fraction; then they drew tight in together, and her cheeks would sink in horribly with each new inhalation. In spite of the ghastliness of it all, that finger would not be withdrawn. I let it lie there across her lips, first blown up and then sucked back in – like some buoy that is tossed about helplessly on the ocean, given an almighty ducking beneath the waves one moment, and suspended aloft like a spinning top on a father's finger the next.

It was only then that I noticed quite how badly she smelled, and I wondered to myself how long it had been so, and whether the children had been as sensitive to her smell when she lay in that caravan as I was now. For some reason, I was overcome with a mixture of fear and shame – fear that they would damn me forever for my neglect of her; and shame that I had not washed her and fed her properly. I saw on the edges of her lips some tiny, encrusted fragments of yellow which I knew to be remnants of the yolk of an egg which she had eaten for her breakfast on that morning she had fallen...

How many days ago had it all happened? I could not fit the pieces together in my mind. Had Deg gone to his maker soon after her tragedy? It seems that my head would not work for me. I hit my face with my hand in a vain attempt to restore my faculties to good order, but it was of no avail. I even went so far as to withdraw the hand which had rested on her face, and apply the knuckles of my index fingers to my own temples. Having put them in position on either side of my head, I shut my eyes, clenched tight my jaws, and screwed the knuckles into my temples with such force that my hands began to tremble with the pressure. It had been a remedy of our old grandmother's for the migraine in bygone days, but it was of no use to me now.

When I opened up my eyes again, her head was bent over that favourite cornflower-yellow dress of hers, and she was smoothing out the hem between her fingers. She worked with such loving care and attention that I swelled with pride just to see her apply herself so. It was not long before she sensed that my eyes were upon her. She giggled into her collar and turned her head half away from me. I believe that she even thrust the knuckle of her thumb into that sweet red mouth of hers to hide her bashfulness at having been watched by me with such devotion.

I could not know this for certain because her back was to me now; but I could see that her heart was light because her shoulders was gently shaking. Surely she was laughing with the pleasure of it all.

'What is it that makes you laugh so, Delphine?' I said back to her. She threw me a half-glance across her shoulder, being careful to hide her mouth with her hand. She observed me closely for a moment or two before she replied. There were indeed tears in those eyes – tears of laughter. Then she dropped her guard. She smiled broadly and boldly at me. It was more than I could ever have expected. My heart leapt.

'I am laughing at you, mister.'

'For why?'

'Because you have spent the whole of this last hour looking at me.'

'And why should that give you so much pleasure, Delphine? Is it some new discovery that I am observing you in this way?'

She cocked her head, a little puzzled.

'You have changed over the months, and for a

long while I didn't believe it. You were once such a boisterous one, with time for nothing but your games and your traps. Now you sit here and watch me, and it is enough for you. Or so it seems.'

'You are right, Delphine. It is enough for me. Why should I wish for more? But is it enough for you? I ask myself. Will you tell me that?'

I reached out to take her hand and she did not stop me.

'It is not a matter of my wishes, mister. I am only a daughter, and a daughter does not decide that sort of thing in our household. You must ask my father. It is he who decides.'

The anger rose in my throat and I released her hand.

When I next took up that hand, all strength had gone from it. I knew that it was not amongst her habits to squeeze my hand or otherwise acknowledge that the pressure of one hand upon another had some meaning... But now all strength had gone from it. It was not difficult to close her fingers upon my hand, and this I now proceeded to do, with extreme care, one by one.

I have heard it said that when the spirit passes out of a body, the limbs set hard so quickly that it is well nigh impossible to change their position. As I stared down at that pale hand enclosing mine, I began to fear that I would have to bear her along with me until eternity – or, at best, that I would be obliged to sever hand from arm and keep the two tucked inside my shirt, close to my heart. This thought tickled me, and I laughed out loud as I released her grip.

After some minutes of hard labour, I had released her frame from the welter of blankets that bound it. Then I proceeded to remove the night dress, her only remaining garment. I drew forth my pocket knife and hacked away at the collar. Soon the knife's blade was sliding easily down the whole length of it, and it only remained to me to peel back the linen. As easy as peeling an orange, I thought to myself blithely. By the little light that stole through the entrance, I saw by my watch that it was coming on to nine o'clock in the evening again. How quickly that whole day had passed by!

I found the candle that I had removed from the caravan, and struck a match on a small stone that lay only inches away from her left hand. It did not fire. Even then some part of me wondered whether the hand which lay there, so limp and so cold, might not yet close around that stone and toss it across the cave – as if in her sleepy state she half-expected that a dog might go after it. But what dog was there here? And what life was there in that hand to lure a dog even if one should appear?

Suddenly, I heard the quick bark of a dog – outside, somewhere, just beyond the entrance. And I smelt some dog's urinous reek too – as it must have smelt mine. I heard its paws beginning to scrabble furiously at the hard, compacted earth.

Clearly, it was too big – or too stupid – to find its way in without digging away at the ground beneath its feet.

Or so I prayed… Quickly and quietly I folded the rendered pieces of cloth back across her naked body, and spread the bandages about in order to conceal her as well as I possibly could. Then I heard a heavy foot strike against a rock – once, twice, thrice.

'Give over that infernal digging, dog, before I brain you with my boot!' The voice was harsh and impatient. Perhaps all would be well after all. Yes, his next words reassured me all the more.

'You crag me up to these god-forsaken haunts of yours.. Are you not satisfied now? Must you forever be digging up the clay? Come now.'

I heard a dull thud and the dog howled. It stopped its digging and seemed to skid away from the entrance, for as it turned to go it thrust backwards with its feet, throwing a handful of earth back into the cave, some morsels of which struck the soles of my shoes.

I had my hands pressed tight together in prayer. I was pleading that they would not find us, that they would leave us in peace again. And so they did. The steps disappeared after the dog, and all was still again. I felt around the cave floor for the match, which surely could not have gone far… I would have lit another without further ado had there not been so few in that box that I could ill afford to waste one. Eventually, my finger closed upon it. I picked it up and lodged it with the utmost care behind my ear. I made a small hole for the base of the candle between her feet, and there I drove it in, shoring it up on all sides with earth and dirt and stones for fear that it would no sooner be alight than it would topple over, and I would have to begin the wasteful business of lighting it all over again.

Before I did the act, I threw aside the outer coverings again, unknotted her hair, spread it in a halo around her head, and re-opened the holy diptych of her night gown.

I lit it then, and knelt down beside her. Now was the moment to offer up to God my prayer of thanksgiving that he would take her to Him at last. She would suffer no more in this world, which was a blessed thing.

I knew as I gazed upon her naked body how right I had been to ignore the warnings of Mr Henderson. That man was indeed a false prophet. The Lord himself had made it clear to me. As soon as the man had spoken of the hospital, I knew that he had failed me – and, much the greater sin, failed his Maker. He had stolen my money; he had abandoned my loved one in her hour of greatest need. Thanks be to God that He had made clear to me the way forward. Without Him, she would have continued to suffer needlessly. I would not easily or quickly forget the misdemeanours of Mr Henderson, that man who was so ready to dispense the teachings of the Almighty from a blue van.

I wondered then whether that Madge would be true to her word. She had deserved the reward of that morsel of cheese; but even such a gift as that might not cause her to cleave to me forever. She was as a skiff that is tossed upon the waves, that one, when it was a matter of displaying loyalty to her own father. Had I not stood beside her and forced her to eat the cheese, she might have shared it with Lenny, and the tongues of the two of them would soon have been flapping to my disadvantage, I doubted not.

'Dearest God,' I said out loud, 'I have the dear one with me now, and I have lit a candle in demonstration of the fact that I am ever your obedient servant – as you have taught me to be.'

It seemed then that I had said all that I had to say, and I must now go about my peaceful business. With great difficulty, I dragged myself out into the fresh air again, and, availing myself of what little light the moon shed upon the earth that night, I began to search for the sticks and larger stones which were necessary to the successful outcome of this holy business. Here and there I came upon limbs of gorse that had been broken off by the tramping of feet and had now, being dead, gone brittle. I swore at the thorns which pricked me, for the pain was sharp and unexpected. He would surely ignore such venial sins; he would see that I was engaged upon a greater act of homage, and a little impatience in the preparation was justifiable and surely to be forgiven.

I heaped all that I could find in a great mound before the entrance, and when I was satisfied that I had sufficient, I knelt beside it and began to break it up, piece by piece, into manageable lengths. And as I broke the pieces, I tossed them into the cave, great and small. The stones also I rolled inside.

Having completed my outdoors task, I drew my body inside again, and set to measuring Delphine with the aid of a long, straight stick that I had chanced upon. Three and one half stick lengths by one and one half – to be on the safe side. I set the stones together, side by side, until I had built a low altar of some five or six inches in height. Without such an altar, the act would not be sanctified, his Word had taught me; and I was determined to obey his strict law to the last, least letter.

I felt proud of those snugly fitting stones when I sat back to examine with pride what I had achieved. There was not so much as a finger's width between any of them. What is more, to the naked eye the altar was nigh on a perfect rectangle – another demonstration of how I had striven to please Him by the perfection of my work.

Having completed the tasks of stone mason and dry-stone waller all rolled up in one – I flattered myself a little, of course – I took up those lengths of stick by the handsful, and strewed them about the stone altar to a depth of some three to four inches, smoothing them out as evenly as my hands would allow. When I ran my hands across the surface for the last time, I found a stick or two projecting straight upwards – or outwards – from the rest at an unacceptable angle. These I broke off and thrust amidst the rest – almost as if I were reminding them that the first would be last, and the one to be exalted would be found amongst the least of these my brethren...

For as I worked, my head was ever stuffed with His words, which would drift in and out of my mind as if spoken by different voices – but each one a facet of that heavenly voice which leans down from above and speaks into the ear as intimately as man speaks to man.

It was a true miracle, and one before which I felt mightily humbled, for at times the words would speak of meekness, humility and human kindness – and at such times the voice would have the soft persuasiveness of velvet. At others, it would tell of my duty to speak his truth to the wrongdoer, and then it would be loud and rasping and fearful, almost as if the blade of a knife were being drawn across a stone beside my ear, back and forth, setting the teeth on edge. But I knew them all for Him, and I thanked Him that He guided me and attended to my every need.

Now it was matter of lifting that dear body onto the altar, and how to achieve that aim without making too much of a disturbance upon the surface of the sticks. I had not intended to make use of the great grey blanket until later, but now I saw that it was necessary to change my plans a little in order to surmount the present difficulties.

As a boy, my father would chastise me for the fact that I was no great fire builder. In our house, it was the duty of the youngest to build the fire in the kitchen hearth, and many were the mornings that the door had swung open and he had found me there, fretting and sneezing amidst the soot and ashes. And was there so much as a glimpse of the least spark in that grate? No, there was not – despite the fact that I may have laboured for half an hour or more to avoid his mockery and heavy chastisements. Yes, many were the mornings that he walked across the kitchen, took me by the ear, and turned me out of that hearth. And there I would lie, sprawled, ears and eyes burning that I had failed him again.

Yet, much as I tried – and tried I did, again and again – I could not seem to learn the skills of the fire maker, and, in my greater age, I came to accept this failing of mine as the will of Almighty God; and having turned over and over in my mind the problem and how best to solve it, I hit upon the simplest of answers, and one, moreover, which has never failed to conceal my deficiencies...

I speak, of course, of that wondrous liquid, paraffin.

I drew the bottle from my outer pocket, removed the screw cap, and sniffed the heady pink liquid, a smell that always pleases me greatly. I made the cap firm again and jumped the bottle up and down in my hand. Ample for the needs of the moment, I thought to myself with satisfaction. Evidently, it had not leaked. There are those who mock me for clinging to the old glass bottle. They tell me that plastic is better and lighter and altogether more reliable. This is not my experience. I cleave to the old ways.

Having laid out the blanket on the floor of the cave, I rolled it up carefully, evenly, and then placed this roll at the foot of the altar. Then I unrolled it all over again and, having smoothed it out to my satisfaction, doused it in the paraffin, making sure that I had spread the liquid evenly across the whole surface. Then I took up the body in my arms – it seems that I was granted strength which I had not hitherto possessed, for which I thanked Him with all my might as I struggled with the burden – and placed it on top of the blanket.

How serene and untroubled she looked at last! No one could do her harm now. She was at last beyond the reach of evil. I have heard say that it is not difficult to close the eyes of the dead; but this one's remained as obdurately open as they had ever been throughout her last days. I crossed the blanket over her again – first the left fold and then the right. Such drops of paraffin as still remained in the bottle, I scattered about the bed of sticks, which I saw, to my satisfaction, had not been overmuch disturbed by the laying of the burden upon the blanket.

All was now as ready as a human hand could make it. Before taking up the box of matches, I placed two twigs – straight and perfect examples of their kind, and the one three times the length of the other – upon the blanket between her breasts. I arranged them one upon the other in the form of a cross. Then I struck the first match, and it caught without a second's hesitation.

I heaved myself out of the cave again as quickly as my limbs would carry me, and once out in the open air, I began to gather up such obstructive materials as I could find to block up the entrance. A number of rocks which had proved too large to be taken inside served my purpose well; and, similarly, several larger limbs of trees helped to make the barricade all the more impregnable. Added to which, of course, came much rubble, green stuff, and so on and so forth. I knew that all was proceeding well within by the distant sound of spitting and crackling, and I glimpsed the occasional flicker of light which even a barrier as mighty as the one I had constructed could not conceal entirely.

The moon was now as full as it would be that night. I stepped back and, straining up, up on my tiptoes, saw that which I had expected to see issuing from the apex of the rocks which formed the walls and the roof of that cave: a thin plume of grey smoke spiralling up into the atmosphere, shifting to left or right as the wind decreed like some dancing genie of the upper air.

I sought out with my eye and, not without some small effort, eventually heaved myself up and into a small crevice in the rock wall which faced the entrance. And there I sat, bemused by that spume of smoke, for a length of time which my mind was not able to measure. Such was my awe, such my sense of gratitude – the gratitude that a son feels towards a father when, with his aid, he has been permitted to accomplish a task which even in his wildest dreams he believed to be beyond him. And yet all *is* possible, I told myself then, if it is His wish that it come to pass.

And it was at that moment that He vouchsafed to me that he could not much longer endure the godless behaviour of Mr Henderson, and that I was to be the instrument of his chastisement. So be it, Lord, my lips muttered almost involuntarily as my eyes continued to stare into the upper air.

How many hours I slept I do not know, but when I awoke – with a start, some hours later – my limbs felt uncommonly stiff and my brow was burning and feverish in spite of the fact that the rain was drumming down heavily upon me and had soaked right through my clothing, including the three pairs of under-trousers I usually wear. I was abnormally shocked by the sight of my right hand, which was fully immersed in a pool of water which had formed in the nook where the hand had come to rest. Why this should be so I cannot tell; but I quickly drew it forth and trapped it in my armpit for a little reviving warmth.

And then a much greater shock left me rigid with fright. I raised my streaming head to the top of the cliff face opposite and saw to my horror that the smoke had disappeared entirely. What, I asked myself, if the rain had fallen in such quantities that the altar had been doused, leaving the body half intact – and as dripping wet as I was at this moment?

Having wiped my face on my sleeve, and shook the water from my hair as well as I was able, I scrambled down from my crevice, and no sooner had I hit solid ground than I groaned from the terrible, jarring impact of hard earth upon those poor, benumbed limbs of mine.

I dragged myself to the entrance, flexing my arms and stamping my feet as I went in a vain attempt to restore life and some feeling to my decrepit frame. Then God must have granted me a renewal of strength, for I began to tear at my barricade like a demon in an absolute frenzy, ripping and kicking and heaving; letting fly with every active limb of my body, the quicker to investigate what had happened – or, my greater fear, had not happened – within. No sooner had I made a hole big enough for my bulk than I plunged inside, taking with me upon my clothes many of the leaves and stones and twigs that had gone to make up that magnificent bulwark.

My body was so wracked by the pain of its singular efforts, and my mind so stuffed with apprehension, that I remained on all fours for a few moments, panting like a dog and praying that my calmer, more rational faculties would soon be restored to me.

By and by the pain eased off a little, and I was able to open my eyes and become aware of my surroundings. I crept nearer and sat back on my haunches. My eyes took in everything at a glance.

I was saved! Such feelings of joy and relief commingled overwhelmed me that I wept into my sleeve and was not able to look again until I had ceased snivelling and dried my eyes. She was quite gone. Quite. The height of the altar had saved me. Never for a moment had I dreamt that it would serve this purpose – but it had and I was saved. I scarcely noticed that I was kneeling in a great pool of water; nor did I think for one moment that my knees would torment me in due course. My crowning obsession was that she was quite blown away – or would be shortly…

With the exception of a fragment or two of bone – which was, of course, piping hot to the touch – I could find nothing as I raked with my hands, back and forth, with exceeding care, but ashes. Dust and smoking ashes. And who would distinguish the ashes of a blanket or a stick from that of a body? All had been reduced to that simple element to which he reduces us all at the last.

I meditated upon this sombre fact as I let a

handful slip through my fingers and back onto the heap. I determined then that I would make a great bundle of the ash and assign it to the waves without delay. It would then be as if it had never been; not a fleck would remain to arouse the least suspicion. My principal concern now therefore was to procure a sack or piece of cloth into which I could heap it all, and one, moreover, which would not catch on fire during the carrying. I must on no account underestimate the heat which those fragments of bone had trapped within them.

I sucked on my burnt finger ends. There was testimony indeed of what harmful consequences could follow the careless act. I sat back on my haunches to consider this problem, and as I did so my body gave an almighty shudder.

There I had it! The answer was closer to me than I could ever have dreamt. The very coat which had protected me so imperfectly from all that sluicing rain was now so sodden through and heavy with water that it would serve my purpose exactly. Without further ado I tore it from my shoulders and began to make an incision in the lining – large enough to enable me to pile the ashes inside.

It was indeed a capacious thing. She had complained often enough how ill it fitted me, and if I did not tailor it to make a better fit, she would cast it out with the rubbish, and that way force me – if it were the last thing she did – to be a more perfect gentleman. Holding it open by splaying out the fingers of my left hand, I began to pile in the ashes with all my might.

I was scooping with such concentrated ferocity that I was not even aware of his presence until his hand suddenly closed upon my shoulder. My fright was such – I believed when I felt that hand touch me that the Devil himself had come to claim me – that I screamed out for blue murder, letting fall coat and ashes in the same instant. I swung round. I knew I must confront him even if it were the last thing I did on this earth. And then I saw him in the gloom, so frightened by my shriek that he had shrunk back to the farther wall, and was sucking his thumb noisily as he stared back at me with wide, fearful eyes.

Above all, I had to calm myself now. It would not do to put such terror into the boy's heart that he escape me and bring them all running. Nor must I keep him here overlong or they might come looking for him and find him here before my work was done. Calm then, mister, I said to myself beneath my breath. Calm yourself then or all will be lost…

'Dorin…' I extended my trembling hand to him. Was it composed now, that voice of mine? I believed so. I believed so. 'Dorin… you gave your old father such a fright clapping me on the shoulder like that without any warning. This is a lonely place, and you should be in your home with the others. Is it not the hour at which you usually eat your porridge? What is that Madge doing neglecting you and letting you slip out of her sight? Who knows what harm could have befallen you in these parts? Here…' I reached out to him. 'Come here to your own father, and let me get a better look at you.'

He pushed himself back against the wall all the harder, and let out a small, frightened cry – like a tiny kitten come to new and strange places. I desisted, biding my time. A few moments later, I leant forward again to take him by the arm. Still he resisted, this time raising his hand to his face and defying me with the sharp point of his elbow.

Why was he so frightened? Then I knew. He was staring at the altar from which a few random wisps of smoke were still rising intermittently. What is more, from time to time a breath of air stirred up the ashes, making them billow into the air like a strange-smelling mist.

'Is it the fire that's upsetting you so, Dorin boy? Don't you let it worry you now. It is nothing. How do you think we survive up here without a fire? It is bitterly cold in this place when night falls – as you know yourself, for you have been here without my permission, have you not, my little rapscallion?'

I pointed to the ashes.

'See how it has gone out. All the fuel is spent. She is searching for more at this moment, your mother, but who knows how far she will have to go to find the dry stuff without which a fire cannot burn? How it has rained in these past hours…' I started to rise to my knees.

'But come now, you must return to your Madge. She will be afraid for your safety when she discovers that you are not with her. Go back to her now, boy, and tell her that your mother is repairing; that she is up and will be home with me shortly. Tell them the good news, Dorin. Tell them that she is mending and I will bring her soon. Go now, boy!'

I shouted these last words and flapped my hand at him, guessing that a little menace would not come amiss. Sure enough, he scuttled out of that cave like a dune crab, and I thanked the Lord for another remission.

I gave it five long minutes or more before I slipped out after him. I edged around the rocks to the head of the path and strained to catch sight of him in the distance. There he was now, moving as fast as ever, a good half mile away already. He would be back at the caravan within the hour. No time was to be lost then, for I had no way of telling that his message of half-sense would not set them all buzzing, and bring them scurrying back up to the cave to discover the worst.

I heaped the rest of the ashes into the lining as fast as my hands would go; and there was no doubting the fact that many a scoop spilled over and onto my person. Still, the scattered remnants of a simple fire would not set them all guessing.

With one of the lengths of rope which had

made fast her ankles, I closed up the hole, having first gathered up all the material in my fist, and lashed the rope around it twice and thrice. For good measure, I found other lengths and bound them cross-wise around the great bundle to give it extra strength. Then I heaved the whole thing into the corner while I set about the last task that remained to me before I must hurry to dispose of it.

I let fly with my feet at the stones, sending them rolling and spinning to different parts of the cave. Many of them I booted towards the entrance. Later I would strew them about the ground outside or toss them down the cliff. I was, however, careful to leave a small circle of them behind so that none would doubt that I had had a fire here to give us warmth and succour at dead of night. And I scraped with the edge of my foot at the ashes, all the better to make it seem that they had scattered out from this small circle willy nilly and had not been strewn about the confines of a greater circumference. When all was over and done, it seemed a pretty pleasing picture, and one moreover that would surely fool the most scrupulous observer.

Having kicked out the remainder of the stones, I began to push that great bundle of ashes out after them. I cannot begin to describe the difficulties which beset me then. First it jammed itself against the roof, and I was obliged to lie flat out and push against it with my feet until the blood vessels in my temples nigh on burst with the pressure. Then one of the lengths of rope persisted in hooking itself to a small projection of rock, and the minutest finger work in the most difficult conditions – my arm doubled back beneath that overhang while my eyes stared ahead in the opposite direction – was required to free it.

At last it was through, and we arrived in the fresh air, that obstinate bundle and I, bloodied – my fingers especially – but triumphant.

I sat back on my haunches the better to take the strain, hooked the coil of loose rope over my shoulder, and rose unsteadily to my feet. Now it is a matter of minutes only, I told myself, before I am rid of this terrible burden. And then I will return to this cave and let the balm of sleep soothe my aching limbs.

It was this sweet dream of future rest that urged my feet down that cliff path, and I thought of nought but this as I stared down at those limbs of mine which carried me forward, step by slow, deliberate step.

It must have been a kind of trance that I was in because one moment I was hearing and seeing nothing, and the next he was upon me, her very own father was upon me. Bent over almost double as I was, it was the black boot I first recognised, the very one which had stepped so lightly upon my shoulder, for a man's footwear lasts a lifetime in this country. Now he was moving stiffly, with the aid of a supple birch stick, but the wiry frame remained, though stooped.

He stood stock still in the middle of that downward path, hanging there as if to bait me.

'So it is you then, mister. A fine person to be confronting at this time of the morning. You have been hiding away some years now, have you not?'

I stared back at him, incensed by the harshness of his words, and adjusted the bundle on my back. 'It is you who have done the hiding. I have been where I have been all these years. You have not chosen to bless us with your presence.'

My voice had crept out of its hiding place, a small, lost thing. Why? Why?

'I would not choose to bless the beast that steals a good man's daughter. Let the animals go about their particular business, I say. We humans have our own affairs to mind…' He paused, and then smiled a sideways smile at me.

'But, to my surprise, I hear a good thing of you, mister. The first, I believe, I have heard a man say of you in my lifetime. And it is for this reason alone that I can bring myself to speak to you…'

He paused again, nodding his head. What next? I thought.

'The daughter has been grievously sick, I understand.'

'Delphine, yes…' I tried to clear my throat. It was some terribly dry. 'She hit her head against the caravan as she fell, and she has been suspended between life and death since that hour, saying and doing nothing. She just lies flat out on her bed, staring…'

'And you have asked my friend Mr Henderson to lay his hands upon her…'

'That is true. Mr Henderson has been about his healing business…'

'That is a good man, Henderson. It is a wise choice, mister. If he cannot do it, the devil must have her. And how is her present condition, mister?'

I took in a breath before replying.

'Steady.'

'Is she speaking yet?'

'That Madge hears her.'

He chuckled and sucked in his breath.

'She is some little devil, that Madge. She would know, she would. It was she who told me of Henderson.'

'Madge come up to tell you?'

This was some pretty news. Now I hated the two of them.

'She is a regular little spy upon you, mister, that Madge. And she do sing most beautifully.'

'I did not know her for a singer.'

'When she warms to you, then she will sing, mister…'

All of a sudden, he struck at the ground with his stick as if it had done him some wrong.

'Well, I cannot be wasting my precious time with the likes of you. But you are right to trust in Henderson – and not those new-fangled hospitals.

Do not let her near those contagious places. It will surely be the end of her.'

I stiffened my back. It was some sore from that bundle which I'd dared not set down.

'I shall not let her near them. You have my word for it.' I never spoke a truer word than that.

He clutched my arm as he drew level with me before passing.

'I think there are worse brutes than you, mister. Be good to her, though she may have crossed me.'

The Outpouring

I was careful not to swing that old coat into the wind for, instead of scattering over the waves, the ashes would have blown back into my face and hair, and that, for some reason I could not abide. I therefore undid it quietly, and let it all sift out into the shallows, making a dusty film which swayed gently upon the surface of the water. I shook and shook until the very last morsel had drained into the sea, and then I tossed the coat and the rope behind me onto the sand, relieved to be rid of them at last.

I cannot explain the terrible void that I felt to be inside me at that moment of outpouring. It was as though where blood once moved, and organs and tissue jostled in the way that a living being does, there now remained but a large, empty, echoing chamber, wholly bereft of light. And I was stumbling about that chamber whose floor shifted constantly, being made of nothing which was recognisable to the touch – neither wood nor stone nor compacted earth.

I eased my feet forward so gingerly, seeking out ever a firm spot on which to place them. And that I never found; or, having found it, the other foot could never safely follow. And so I lurched dangerously, nearly toppling over, and saving myself only by the backward whirling of my arms.

And the shouting helped me also. Not that I heard it at all, for my ears were unaccountably blocked; but I felt the vocal chords vibrate, the air rush forth from me, and the mouth strain open as far as it would go. And my eyes blinked open and shut again, my features creased in accompaniment to the reeling body. And I held my arm over my eyes, for some part of me feared that a sudden, searing light would burn out my eyes out altogether and that I would never see again. Not that I could see Him now, of course, no matter how long I dawdled in that chamber, for my eyes always opened upon a greater darkness than my true senses had ever known before.

And I was drenched in self-pity on account of my size, which was exceedingly small in proportion to the vast dimensions of the chamber. I told myself that this was a matter of no consequence; that I was no smaller than in former times; and that the roof of the void which I knew for a chamber was nothing more than the immeasurable dimensions of the night sky.

I was, nevertheless, quite unable to convince myself that such reasonable things as these were true. And then a final accursed trick was played upon me. Suddenly, the ground beneath my right foot fell away, and I was plunged into a liquid from which it seemed that I would never escape. I blew it out of my mouth in hectic desperation and drew it in again through my nostrils. I flailed my arms about all the more furiously, and thrust my head up in a last desperate effort to escape.

And I found myself, having forced my eyes open again, threshing about in the sea. And all the ashes which I had poured forth with such stealth and quietness had washed back over me and were clinging to my arms, my shoulders, my head and – even to my eyelids. And they were washing in and out of my mouth, no matter how quickly I tried to spit them forth, such was my disgust. And I retched violently, mixing the dregs from my lower stomach with the ashes of that woman.

Yet now at least I was conscious again, and I had somehow escaped from that terrible mud bank into which I had fallen. Dragging myself to another part of the sea, I tore off the rest of the clothing which still clung to me, and plunged naked into the water, head and all, praying that by this true act of baptism, I would rid myself of all the evil which still clung to my body.

Having thoroughly abluted, I let my exhausted body drift through the sea parallel with the shore line, exercising only my toes or elbows to keep me afloat. And, little by little, I drifted into the calm of a cove which I took to be within sight of no cliff-top vantage point or human habitation. And here I dragged myself forth onto the sand, and, being free of the water, I collapsed and fell immediately into a sleep heavier than death, praising Him, as I fell, for this unlovely deliverance from all my torments.

I could not guess what hour of the night it was

when I awoke; nor whether I had slept through one whole day or two or more. When I first regained my senses, I was struck with a terrible fear that I might still be wandering about that chamber, but as I touched my limbs and bit on my fingers with my teeth, I knew little by little that that could not be so, and that I had suffered no permanent harm.

Then I thought of those other servants of God who have undergone trials and torments for His sake; and I thanked Him that at no point had my faith in Him wavered – nor His in me, I doubt not. His way is not an easy one, I told myself. And as I examined my chilled and naked body, I was reminded of his words: that no man should store up riches for himself on this earth where moths and rust are liable to corrupt them. And then I was pleased to be rid of those clothes, and I vowed that if He desired his witness to walk naked upon this earth for ever after, I would obey his command like a true and faithful servant.

Yet as I shivered, a voice came to me that clothed I must be, and I set off on my return journey to that caravan and those helpless, sleeping children.

Though it were fully dark, I sought not to expose myself to the solitary night walker by marching boldly and unashamedly upon well trodden paths. Instead, I dodged and veered to left and right, snatching what shelter I could from rocks and bushes and stunted trees. And when

there was no protection ahead, I crawled at speed –
like a beast on all fours – for the night air was
bitterly cold about my person. And from time to
time I paused to rub myself vigorously – chest and
thighs and feet; or to clap my hands about my
torso, flapping like some silly mechanical bird. But
what mattered that my antics looked ridiculous? I
must gain my destination unharmed – and no other
thing was of the least concern to me at that hour.

As I approached that clearing behind the
dunes, I slowed to a cautious crawl, easing my
limbs forward, darting my head this way and that,
and stopping when I feared that I had made a small
disturbance. Nothing stirred within, it seemed. All
was still – the windows blank, and the door quite
shut against the world.

Would they be sleeping side by side on the
floor? Or would Lenny and that Madge have taken
the big bed for themselves, lording it over the
others while their parents were elsewhere? I
ascended the steps of the caravan like a stealthy
dog, knee following hand, and hand, knee. And,
gingerly, having reached that topmost step, my
hand reached out for the knob of the door.

As my fingers closed upon it, I asked myself
whether she would have locked it with the key
which hung on the wall. Had she done so, there
would be nothing else for it but to rap on the
window and surprise them all with my nakedness.
This was not to be desired, I told myself. A naked

father commands less authority than a clothed one; and it was important that the Madge did not usurp my authority, or have an occasion to turn them against me. Nor would I wish to frighten them, or have them think me some strange apparition to be jeered at and mocked.

All these matters I pondered, and again pondered, as my fingers closed upon the wooden knob of that flimsy door. It turned easily and noiselessly. Then I began to push the door inwards – at first ever so gently in order not to stir up a great commotion. I had to be careful not to let the wind thrust it inwards unexpectedly, causing it to swing back with a hard slap against the inner wall...

No, all was well... I rejoiced inwardly as the door opened, and the moon threw a shaft of light across the floor some twelve or eighteen inches long. I held the door steady in my grip and listened. I could not hear a single human sound – neither the gentle, regular breathing of a sleeping child nor the shifting and shuffling of a body beneath its covering.

I wondered to myself why this should be so. Perhaps that terrible experience of mine in the sea, when I was wholly at the mercy of the waves which had played with my person as if I were some doll to be tossed from hand to hand by a careless child, had stopped up my ears, and done damage beyond repair to those delicate organs. I muttered a quiet word to myself, first holding my hand up to my face to prevent the sound's drifting inside. No, I could hear myself all right. All seemed to be well with the faculties of speech and hearing.

I eased the door open a little more and, drawing both my knees onto the top step, I placed a hand flat on the floor where the moonlight fell, and pushed my head around the door. Thanks be to God! I saw once again those mounds of blankets which I had been so accustomed to seeing from our bed. Then I raised my head a little more to examine who, if anyone at all, was sleeping on the marriage bed. Sure enough, the blankets were heaped up in way which suggested human occupancy. I paused again and listened out once more for their breathing. Still I heard nothing. Eventually, convinced now that I would not retrieve my clothes without waking up at least some of those sleeping children no matter what I may earlier have imagined, I rose to my knees, and thence stood up fully and gazed down upon the bed. To my astonishment, no head lay upon those pillows.

Where were the bodies of my most precious children? In panic, I snatched up the topmost blanket to find them – but the bed was quite empty. Quite empty. Beneath that blanket, others were piled in some state of disarray. This discovery pleased me somewhat – and calmed me a little. They had not violated the marriage bed after all. These obedient children were perhaps after all sleeping in their accustomed places on the floor…

But were they? When the doubt struck me, my body felt all clammy with sweat. I moved swiftly across the floor to where their bed linen was arranged in its rows. I lifted up the first blanket gingerly – it was a heap of clothes without an owner. And each bed told the exact same story. Its sleeper had vanished. They had been brazenly snatched from me. I was struck dumb with dismay. Who had stolen these babes from their cradles? Was the Evil One holding them against some ransom? Would they be returned to me if I offered up my soul? Had my faithful obedience to the Lord led to this in the end? Was I a mere pawn in that eternal war between good and evil?

But no – I struck my forehead violently with the hoof of my hand – I knew that I must not doubt Him. Everything has a purpose, I said out loud to myself, beating those evil insinuations from my tortured brain with my fist. I told myself to be calm, and to think clearly.

First, then, He seemed to say: clothe thyself, my servant. Clothe thyself. I obeyed him meekly by rummaging beneath the marriage bed for the Sunday trousers, the best white shirt – I had no thought for the stiffened collar at such a time as this – and the creaking black shoes.

Now fully clothed, I sat down and waited on Him. The next word that came to me was that I must seek out a candle and light it. I duly found one and lit it. 'Now I am illuminated and ready, Lord,' I whispered – the more to offer comfort to myself than to communicate with Him, I feared.

No sooner had the candle shed its wavering light across the surface of our old, pitted table top than I saw the paper, which had been folded neatly upon itself and then folded again. A determined hand has folded this sheet, I said to myself as, pursing my lips, I lifted it up to my eyes. It had no mark upon it but a simple cross – or was it a kiss? Perhaps it was, after all, a kiss… That which it contained would answer this question, surely.

I unfolded it and, laying it flat out on the table, smoothed it with the palm of my hand. No sooner had I done so than I noticed that the message was written in pencil in a large, childish hand. Fearful that I would obliterate the message altogether if I continued to rub back and forth across the surface of the writing, I turned it over and began all over again. When I had ironed out all those creases, I took up the sheet and held it up to the light.

It was that Madge who had done it, for I saw at the bottom of the page how she had written her name boldly and clumsily. I read it aloud to myself, the better to understand what she had to say to me.

Father, you will see when you return that we have quite vanished from our home. Be not afraid for us. No one has kidnapped us or done us ill in any way whatsoever. We will come back to you soon. A man has told us that we cannot feed and protect ourselves without you. He was very concerned for us and urged us fiercely to go to his house and live with him until you brought her back to us. Our mother Delphine will understand why we had to go with him. She will not scold us for leaving this place. Nor must you, my father. I have said nothing to Mr Henderson in disobedience of your wishes. Be happy that I am your dutiful daughter.

Dorin was some frightened, poor boy, when he appeared again. He spoke a very few words, but none that could be understood. He is with us also, and the man has put him to bed and kept him there. He says he has been too much exposed to the damp and the dark and the cold for his own good. Do not worry over him. Already he is inclined to crawl again, and now he opens his eyes fully, which he would not do before. Lenny is reading to us every night as you would wish. The man has chosen a new place in the Bible for our readings. Now it is all about Jesus and his disciples. We love these readings and we do not fail to listen. And every one of us has his own separate chair, and we sit all together in a room with a fire. Do not ask me who this man is for I cannot tell you now. He promises me that he will come to you and tell you where we are so that you will not be anxious over your children. He has a car, this one, and mother will perhaps return to us in it. He will bring this letter to you and leave it on the table where you will find it. The woman has called me to bed, and I am going now.

Your Madge'

And then, squeezed beneath her name, I saw that she had written a message to me in a smaller hand. It was something that she had not remembered to ask or to tell me – but which weighed upon her mind evidently. When I had read the words, I could not believe that they were really ones that she had written. They had no meaning for me. I read them again to assure myself that I had not misread them. But no, they were truly present, and I must make of them what I could.

'Our brother Deg is indeed in Camborne. The man has told me so. He has had word from him today by the fish man, who met another whose wife gave him food and lodging in Redruth. My brothers and sister were clapping and cheering when I gave them the good news. They formed a ring and danced frenziedly, shouting and skipping around the man, who laughed heartily at our pleasure. This day is completely full of happiness now, and when our mother Delphine is with us, all will be together again. It is as though we have been living in darkness, and now the light has come back to us. Deg, the man says, comes to us on Sunday after chapel, and tomorrow I shall wash all the clothes of the children so that they are clean and bright-faced to be embraced by him.'

I dropped the note, but continued to stare at it until the words upon the paper blurred and became a nonsense to me. I repeated over to myself what she had written, slowly and deliberately, as if my mind were a turning wheel, and the words returned as long as the wheel continued to revolve, and there was no way to put a stop to its revolutions...

It was – it must be – nonsense; but it was a persistent, painful nonsense like a dog that clings to the leg and will not be shaken free no matter how many times or in what direction or how vigorously the leg is agitated. That the Deg who had died at my hands should be returning to his brothers and sisters, all dressed in his Sunday best, and be kissing them one by one upon the cheek, was beyond the scope of human reason to comprehend.

I raised my hands over the table and, closing my eyes, made as if to release those vigorous legs of his and, in the mind's eye, I watched his young head plummet into the pool and buffet against the rocks beneath.

The Journey

I snatched the paper from the table, made a tight ball of it in my fist, and hurled it into the corner. My throwing arm hung suspended, trembling, in the air. Sometimes I know myself for a naive creature. This was such a moment. It could not be destroyed, that message. It was in entire possession of my head. Indeed, it made so great a clamour within that there was no space left for another thought, no matter how small and meek and deserving of attention.

Was she indeed the author of my present pain? Had my very own daughter, in her quiet, beseeching insolence, deliberated upon these matters before she wrote? And had she written this letter especially to cause me torment? Or had the hand of another – that man whom she described as their benefactor – guided her own? Was she at the mercy of the whims of this madman? And if this were so, was it not my duty to rescue her – to rescue them all – from his grasp?

So many thoughts were swimming there, each one colliding with and in part thwarting the other. Perhaps it was a careful stratagem hatched between the two of them to entrap me. Perhaps she had run back to the old man, who had piped and smiled and beckoned to them through the window. Had he known – or guessed – what I had been bearing with me in that bundle? Yes? No?

At the last, I persuaded myself to believe in the innocence of my Madge. She would not write such things of her vanished brother if she did not believe them to be wholly true. And my head was so alive with the image of those dancing, circling children that I could not but conclude that it was he – the old man – who had bewitched my poor, innocent babes, and that God was now beseeching me to wrest them from his grasp. He had deceived them indeed, and he must have guessed that his message would bring me running. So I must by all means be circumspect. Any carelessness on my part could not but result in their bodily harm – and my certain capture...

Having thrown aside my clothes, I fell across the marriage bed and drew the heaped blankets over my nakedness. Let sleep overwhelm me, I prayed. Let it be my balm and succour, I pleaded. Without a freshening, healing draught I would not be equipped to go about my worldly business. I was filled with such a dread of continuing wakefulness that I strove to dispel my fears by murmuring out loud words of comfort from the Holy Book.

I meditated upon that Psalm in which the shepherd leads his flock through the valley of death and darkness. But soon this meditation dissolved into a nightmare in which I, the naked man in his bed, awoke to find himself a trussed sheep. And, lying on my back in that bed, I believed myself to be hanging suspended by the legs from a pole, all four legs tethered together, two by two, and below, the fire, which would roast me to perfection, was growing in intensity as boughs were tossed at random into the flames by those who loitered there, chattering idly, laughing, and, from time to time, spitting into that raging heat.

Suddenly, I felt a gob of spit upon my eye, and I strove to blink it open to enable me to see again. Except that the gob of spit was not, I feared, simple saliva, but the steaming hot fat which, when it mingles with water, explodes in the open pan, burning hands, wrists and face in its intensity. And when I felt it drip onto my eye, I fought to release myself from my bonds by swinging my trussed body from side to side and straining with all my might. I feared that if I did not succeed in releasing myself, the eye would be quite burnt out within seconds. But how could such a dumb, fettered animal as I resist?

I fought and fought and, blinking suddenly awake, found that my arms were struggling to free themselves from the blankets which I had knotted about my wrists during all the restless writhing of that nightmare-torn sleep. And my eye was indeed wet with liquid. But when the next drop fell, I knew it for rain water which was seeping through the roof and dripping upon the pillow.

And outside, the morning sky was low and grey and broody with thick cloud, and the rain was falling so heavy, and the winds blowing so strong, that it was as if this flimsy caravan were being tossed upon a storm-wracked sea and would soon be quite destroyed.

I rose up from my bed and picked at my clothes like some desultory ghost, and when I was dressed again in my best, I opened the door of the caravan and drew in a sharp breath of damp morning air. It was a testing time ahead indeed. I would first make my way to the old man's house and, concealing myself in a coppice until dark, I would then strive to rescue my charges – if they were indeed to be found there. The close watch that I would keep upon the house throughout the rest of this dreary day should serve to confirm – or deny – my worst fears.

It was some five miles or more to that village, and I did my best to cleave to the high, concealing hedges as I walked. I saw few men or vehicles upon the lanes that day, and when I discerned one approaching, I turned my back upon him and made myself busy in the undergrowth, delving after a nest or plucking a stray primrose or two for my buttonhole. I have never been a favourite of these people hereabouts, and the less they talk of seeing me about their lanes, the better for the business.

There was a time when Delphine had her societies and such like frivolities, but these I quickly banished, and she was all the more studious for it later. Such friends as she once had slipped from her also, but the loss of them she did not often regret, having children enough and to spare for a single pair of toiling hands…

I slipped quietly behind the wall of the homely kitchen garden whose gate faces the front of that man's house, and there I squatted and watched throughout that whole long day beneath a shady creeping ivy of my choice. I had concealed myself here in times past when first I courted her. I would watch in envious silence as they emerged – father, mother, sisters, brothers – in full spate of human chatter from the black front door whose porch was overhung with cloying wisteria, a slow-creeping thing that evidently delights the senses of mankind to distraction. All was fresh and new to me then, and I would hang about that sequestered place in watchful expectation of some sighting of my dear quarry, keen-scented and taut of limb as a common poacher. He was always with her, that father of hers, as if some special sense told him that if he did not cling fast and cleave to her, she would be spirited away from him forever – as, indeed, it befell.

It happened one sun-struck Sunday morning, lazy with heat ripples. He had preceded her down the lane to the chapel, letting her trail in his wake, suspecting, fearing nothing, quite the master of his territory. With one swift bound, I was over the wall and had her by the wrist. Although she was already my covert lover, and there was an understanding between us, I had shown nothing but insolence to that father of hers, and this deeply grieved her, I knew.

When I caught her, she made as if to cry out and run back to the shelter of the house, but my eyes shone with such a fierce determination, and my hand sealed her mouth with such violence – a gesture which seemed to say: call him at your own peril, Delphine! – that the shock of it all robbed her body of its strength, and she collapsed across my shoulder like a poor rag doll. And thence up the lane, across the field, and into the waiting cart.

Thereafter, she was so tender, meek and compliant, never uttering one word of father, mother or home, that I believed her to be quite satisfied with our pinched lot. I do not doubt that it was my godliness, shining forth in her presence, that caused her to cleave to me. There are men upon this earth who can offer to womankind little more than manly pride. This man lacked not such pride, but he also stood upon a high rung of the golden ladder which stretches up from earth to heaven, and beckoning her up to him. And in her womanly meekness, she obeyed.

Such comfortable thoughts as these trickled down through my brain as I squatted beneath the ivy and watched for them.

Soon after midday, the blue van turned into the lane which separates house from kitchen garden, and stopped before that great black front door. This I watched with great interest, even raising my head above the wall because now, at a stroke, I had lost my easy view of both door and porch. I saw Henderson's great bulk heave itself from the driver's seat, stand upright in the lane, glance to left and right, adjust its hat, and clear its throat.

The healer drew from some deep inner pocket of his cloak a thin silver blade that flashed momentarily in the sunlight. The sudden appearance of this blade perplexed me. What could be the purpose of such a thing? And why draw it forth in the road? Had he some evil intent that I should presently witness? But no, it seemed not, for he drew the silver blade across his nail and back again, back and forth like a fiddler wielding some tiny bow. But there was no accompanying sound of music; nothing but the scratch of blade upon nail, paring it back until he judged it to be perfectly shaped.

I wondered how a man of God could be absorbed by such vanities; but when I recalled how he had tricked and failed me, it seemed no great surprise that such frivolous activities should engage his attention. Having completed the sawing of every nail to his satisfaction, he slipped the instrument back into his cloak, dusted the parings from the swell of his stomach, and cleared his throat again.

Then he approached the door with the breezy confidence of a man who has just now arrived at his destination, and has not hesitated for one single second. Of such stuff is human duplicity made. He who has observed him from the window will know better, I told myself. And then I experienced a sudden chill. If Henderson's antics had been witnessed, it was possible that I too had been observed in my observing of him...

I drew myself down below the top of the wall again; but within the space of a second or two, my intense curiosity had driven me back up again. For, having heard his firm rap upon the door, I was determined to see what manner of man or woman would open up to him, and whether anyone else would be visible behind in that very passageway where I had stood in such a state of unhappy indecision so long ago...

He waited for a few moments, nervously squeezing one palm against the other as he glanced idly around. Then he knocked again. This time it was firmer, louder, and the number of raps six (I counted every one). He seemed determined to rouse them no matter what. The hair atop my head fair bristled with apprehension. But there was still no response.

He stepped back from the porch and stared up at the windows of the second storey which the sun's dazzle had made it difficult for the eye to penetrate. He looked to left and right, missing the central window for it was blind – a mere painted, window-like space to please the eye by its symmetry. Now he squatted down on his haunches, a difficult feat for one of such a bulk. He groaned as he lowered himself, which caused me to smile a little. Then, taking up a handful of earth, he stood up again and threw some fragments at the left-hand window and some at the right.

He watched and waited, and I busied myself in like manner behind him. Those dimpled panes of glass would deceive the most curious eye, I thought, for the light shifted so upon their surfaces, bulging like a bubble one moment, tapering like an hour glass the next; and, at yet another, assuming a form so human that my heart began to beat all the harder… Could it be my Lenny or my Jamie that I recognised, peeking out at this unexpected visitor, but doing so with such caution that only I – and not he – could see them watching him?

But it was all mere fantasy, I knew, for soon that familiar face would elongate itself unnaturally, nose and chin disappearing entirely, and I would resign myself to the fact that the light had been up to its old tricks again.

One time a morsel of earth fell back and rapped him smartly on the brim of the hat, which caused him to half-turn towards me, face flushed with anger. I flushed back in response – it had seemed for all the world that he was scowling at me. But no, it was merely the falling earth that had roused him.

Seeing that all this throwing and knocking was to no avail, he pulled his cloak about him and turned away as if preparing himself to return to the van again. Then, thinking otherwise, he drew a pen and a piece of paper from his pocket and proceeded to scribble a hasty message. Twice he interrupted his scribbling to look at his watch. The harassed face, the movement of the lips, the fixed, concentrated stare, the speed with which the pen wove back and forth – all this made it plain to me that he had to be away just as quickly as the vehicle could carry him as soon as this tiresome job was done.

He folded the paper and disappeared into the porch. My clear view of him was now blocked by the van, but the noise of the sliding of paper told me that he must be pushing it beneath the door. Then he returned to the van, the engine coughed and spluttered a time or two, and he was off, leaving only a cloud of dust in the air by which to remember him – and, of course, that note beneath the door which I could now plainly see.

I was debating hotly within myself whether or not to retrieve the note when, to my astonishment, the old man limped hurriedly around the side of the house with a grim expression on that part of his face which was not shaded from the sun by an old grey cap. He was brandishing a pair of ancient hedge-clippers, and I feared for his straggling ends of privet. How was it that he had caught neither sight nor sound of Henderson though? And if Henderson and he were indeed such boon companions, how was it that the healer had not troubled to seek out his friend and neighbour at the back of the house? Would he not have taken tea many a time beside that hob? Whatever the reason, it was clear that the old man knew nothing of the visit, and was wholly absorbed in the contemplation of his raggedy privet hedge and the feeble-minded dog rose that toiled up the trellis of his porch.

No sooner had he begun to pick at the trailing branches, pushing them through the holes in the trellis or snapping them off altogether if they had served their purpose, than his eye caught sight of the note. He plucked it from underneath the door (quite surprising me with his nimbleness), stuffed it straight into his pocket, and then went on with the pruning. So that is how important the note is to him! I thought to myself with no small irritation.

Now there was little more to be seen, and so I sat back down to bide my time. When the click-clack of the shears ceased, I would look again. I drew from my pocket a fresh egg, and, pricking the shell, sucked out its insides. It was the first refreshing food of the day. The sun warmed me; God had fed me; and a little inner contentment began to steal back into my body.

But it was not to last. Just then, my ear caught a distant grumble of thunder, and drops of rain began to fall, each one so large that it disturbed the earth on which it fell or made the grass blades bend and flick.

The shears fell silent. I raised my head again and watched him stumble around the corner of the house towards the back kitchen, bearing the shears across his shoulder. With the other hand he pulled vigorously at the brim of his cap. And with every step that he took, he cursed. And then I saw it. In his haste to escape the oncoming storm, he must have pulled his waistcoat about him too abruptly... Yes, there was the note, plainly visible on the ground, shifting and twitching in the dousing rain. I quickly ran out, crouching as I ran, and snatched it up from the shallow puddle in which it lay. And as I hurried back to my retreat, I shook the worst of the rain water from it.

This was a lucky stroke indeed. I devoured his words with my eyes. 'Violet will be at the organ on the morrow,' he had written in his thin, small hand, 'you can rest assured of it. There is no one in this country who plays a more rousing Easter hymn. But she must needs eat some of your dinner. I hope that you will not begrudge it. And if you keep her for the afternoon and the procession, she will take a bite of your Easter tea into the bargain. Let us all pray for a fine, uplifting day — for ourselves and all God's children everywhere.'

I had lived so much in my head, and the days had come and gone so speedily, that even the day of the Resurrection of our Lord had nearly passed me by without my noticing! I was so humbled by this chance discovery that I fell to my knees and begged his forgiveness. Would it ever be thus? Would I always live this hermit's life, knowing nothing of the greater world outside except by the chance reading of some message on a paper which one human being sends to another – but seldom to me? Such pitiful thoughts assailed me that I wept openly as I contemplated my loneliness. But no man is truly alone, I soon chided myself, and especially not I who am so beloved of my Maker. And then I scolded myself sharply for the ease with which I had declined into self-pity, and I began to ponder a little more upon the words that Henderson had written to the old man.

I began to imagine to myself how the children would process, with all due solemnity, up the hill from the chapel, behind the one who would be bearing that gorgeous, flapping Sunday School banner. And at the very moment when their hearts and minds were most fixed upon the Lord and his blessed Resurrection, Deg would step smartly from the hedgerow, grinning, ragged as a scarecrow, and greet them all, faces flushed and smiling, with a tender brotherly embrace. Jamie would hang from his leg, straining back and near on toppling the boy, begging to be taken up into his arms. Lenny would catch him about the waist and press her sharp little nose into his warm stomach. Dorin would crawl round and round, weaving in and out of his big brother's legs if they were sufficiently splayed, yelping like a playful pup whose master has returned from his day labours at last. And Madge would tie her arms around his neck, filling his ears with news of all these strange occurrences of late –

how their mother had hit her head and come to grief, and had been taken away, trussed up like a bundle of old rags for the chapel jumble sale; of how I had admonished her sternly and left her to guard the little ones, and what a burden it had all been to her; and how she had cried, unsleeping, over their exhausted bodies; and how the man had startled them all by banging open the door and calling them away to the comfort of his home, or surely they would otherwise have perished; and of how he had told them over a most wondrous breakfast of heaped up toast larded (front and back most like) with real yellow cow's butter, that he, their most beloved brother, would be returning to them on Easter Sunday; and of how they had created such a hullabaloo in that kitchen, stamping and jumping and dancing around, that they had nearly turned the kettle off the hob and grievously scalded themselves.

But, happily, they had in truth done no such thing, and now he was with them as the old man had solemnly promised; and their joy knew no bounds for they had missed him so – oh, how they had missed him!

And ruddy-faced Deg would raise his head and, looking her straight in the eye, ask where exactly their father was at this minute, for he must have urgent conversation with him concerning their poor mother…

Part Two

Phantasmagoria

But no, no, no… He shook his head violently to left and right, and clapped his hands over his ears. These images were surely the devil's handiwork, and he would have no truck with such unholy nonsense.

Now, in the cool of the evening, he raised his head above the wall again and stared up at those blank windows. A light, refreshing breeze stirred the hairs of his head, and a new lightness of spirit returned to him. He wiped his hands across his mouth and spat at the ground beside his feet…

The drapes of the upper windows had now been drawn against the oncoming dark and, as he looked, the window areas filled to the brim with light, first one and then another. He made out the shadow-profile of a figure of medium height, and he watched as it raised its arm up to the curtain. Then several fingers appeared between the curtains, tugging them ever more closely together. They are afraid of letting their light escape or of letting that which is outside see what is happening within, he told himself. It was undoubtedly the slender hand of a woman which had adjusted that curtain. That Madge, he guessed, could not have reached so high – except by standing on a chair, and this he would surely have seen. The same hand tugged again at the curtain in the left-hand window, but this time fewer fingers appeared. The gap between those curtains was not so great, he cleverly surmised.

Then his attention was caught by the outer

door's scraping open. The old man appeared in the doorway, glanced hastily to left and right, then, falling to his knees, he felt this way and that beneath the mat which lay on the threshold in the shade of the porch. The kneeling man drew forth a stout black key and, rising to his feet again, he retired into the passageway, pushed and scraped the door shut, and fumbled the key into the lock. The lock went home with a click and the key was withdrawn.

The man looked grim and nodded his head. It is the back way then, he murmured to himself. Having first listened and looked for any signs of movement, human or animal, up or down the lane, he threw his leg over the wall of the kitchen garden, and with two quick, light steps reached the gate which guarded the way to the porch. He pushed it open without further ado, having already taken note of the fact that it had opened silently for Mr Henderson. He had known that that would assist him later.

He was slipping noiselessly around the side of the house, congratulating himself upon his fleetness of foot and suppleness of limb, when he felt a sudden tug at his jacket. He whirled around, fearful, but poised as ever to deal with this latest threat to his person. As it happens though, the enemy was a phantom one: in cleaving to the wall of the house, he had let his coat rub up against stone, and – cursed be that man! – a rusting nail that supported the thread which guided the trailing dog rose had caught on and pulled at his jacket.

Free again, he hurried on, and, having stepped over and around a motley assortment of buckets and tubs that were strewn about the cobbled path up to the back door, he reached his destination. He had rightly guessed that the back of the house would be in darkness now. But first he stopped to listen out for any sound of movement within – who knows but at this very moment the old man, dropping his book, might not have decided to go to his kitchen to black his working boots, remembering that no hand was to be lifted in toil on the morrow? No. Not a scrape. Not a cough. Not a rustle.

He put his thumb on the latch and his fingers around the handle of the door. He pressed, and the latch rose with a gentle click. Pulling back on the handle, he pushed forward with his knee – but to no avail. After budging no more than a quarter of an inch, the bolts at top and bottom held it fast. He pulled back and pushed forward again once or twice, but soon abandoned all hope. Stepping back from the door, he jammed hands on hips and cursed his ill luck.

It is shut fast against me and my kind, he brooded. And yet he was not quite defeated yet. His eyes roamed up the side of the old cob wall of the back kitchen – and there he spied it. A poky window in the second storey was slightly ajar. He watched it sway back and forth a little on its hinge.

How surprising that the old man should have overlooked it! Yet was he himself capable of reaching it? He was. He had to be.

Finding handholds in the pitted wall, he began to climb until his hands closed upon the window sill. But then it seemed as if he could go no further. It was as though his very legs had lost all hope. They slipped out of every new foothold, and floundered helplessly in the air. Even the window sill seemed to be crumbling to pieces in his hands, such was the age of the cob. Gradually, painfully, he felt himself slide back down the wall until his feet again reached the sill of the ground-floor window. And from there he jumped clear away from the path, and onto the grass.

He lay panting and dispirited for a little while; but soon he picked himself up and retraced his steps to the kitchen garden. Creeping beneath the ivy again, he curled up like a wounded animal and fell asleep, exhausted by his painful, fruitless efforts.

Resurrection Day

It was the old man's shouting voice that awoke him with a start. He blinked awake and saw that the sun had already risen. He raised his head to discover the reason for all the commotion. The old man was standing beside his gate, brandishing a key in his fist, and shouting to some other that he had found what was missing – but what good was it appointing a new keeper of the chapel if, on his very first Sunday – and not just any Sunday either, but one of the most important in God's calendar – the boy – yes, boy he called him, but the man could see when this so called boy came into view, all red-faced with embarrassment, that he was not a day less than twenty years old if he was a day – lost his key and had to get the old man up from his bed to scratch around for the replacement which, as luck would have it, was to hand?

The old man made as if to strike the new keeper with the spare key, but when the lad drew back in terror, holding his hands up to his face to save himself from injury, the other one began to laugh, and strike the key repeatedly against his palm.

'Let this be a lesson to you then, Ginger, not to trouble me again at this hour. Now be off and do your work or the chapel will not be ready for the service.'

Ginger, half crouching and touching his cap,

extended his hand, and, thanking the old man over and over again, retired meekly, mumbling to himself as he trudged back down the lane, shoulders hunched, the way he had come. The old man watched him go, hands on hips and sneering at his back. Then he tut-tutted loudly and turned briskly on his heel, a new authority in his step. The door slammed shut and the peace of Easter Sunday returned to the lane.

But not for long. For no sooner had the man settled himself down comfortably again than the shrieks of children's voices broke the silence, and he thrust his eager head above the wall again to seek out the source of the noise. He noticed that the upper windows of the house were now wide open – but the blowing curtains prevented his seeing who was within. He tried his best to distinguish the different voices that were speaking or shouting, but it seemed that they were all talking at the same time – and, what is more, several deeper voices were now mixed in with the general youthful clamour.

And then a sudden silence fell, followed by a prolonged hooray, which was repeated several times. And this was soon succeeded by the most thunderous burst of applause, which was itself accompanied by a great rumbling as if many pairs of feet were drumming upon the floor-boards. And when all this general clamour ceased, a single voice could still be heard, undoubtedly male this time, but not so deep or so mature as the earlier ones had been.

He strained to catch the words which were

being spoken, but a most dreadful thought was now in full occupation of his mind again. Could it be true what she had said? Did he – or did he not – recognise the voice as that of his dead son Deg?

The words came clearer now. It was almost as if the speaker had stepped a little closer to the window in order to make sure that his words would be heard outside. But why would he torment me thus? the man asked himself as the clear words drifted down from the window and into his straining ears like so many dandelion clocks borne on the wind…

'It is the day for which we have all been waiting… And on this day the good Lord did for himself what he had done for Lazarus, that man who died but lived again by the grace of the living God…'

Lazarus! The man listening in the garden could not believe that he had heard the name spoken. What was he doing, that Deg, to use the name of Lazarus against his own father, God's most faithful servant? Had that Madge told him everything then – even down to what he had said to them before they bundled her up and away? Or were his ears deceiving him?

He glowered up at that window again. Could Deg really and truly be present in that upper room? It must surely be the devil's work, he concluded, for it is said that the devil clothes himself in the likeness of God and his servants, the better to taunt the godly and lead them astray…

He stared down at the palms of his hands, encrusted with mud and soil as they were, and asked of his hands whether they were ready and willing to do God's business. He flexed his fingers, one by one, and asked of them all individually whether they were strong to do the Lord's bidding. Show me then that you can be trusted, he whispered to his servants, those hands, and at his bidding the left one rose up to his throat and pressed and pressed with all its might until he had to shout aloud: 'Enough!' And the coughing fit that followed left him so breathless that he could no longer listen to the voice of the boy behind that upstairs window because of his own raucous panting.

But when his breathing stilled, he could hear the voices of the children again, sharp and clear as the daylight that now bathed his own body, and they were singing at the tops of their young voices words that he knew from of old, and the last few of these – 'We all fall down!' – were shouted in hysterical unison. And as they all sang that single word 'down!', there was an almighty thunder of falling bodies, and the singing dissolved again into wild shrieks of laughter.

Feeling greatly displeased to hear them dancing such wild, pagan dances on the Lord's Resurrection Day, he laid all caution aside and sprung up from behind the wall, fully determined now to put a stop to all this nonsense, and to seize back his charges from the devil's clutches. He marched boldly across the road and kicked open the gate that led to the porch. Then, having cleared a path for himself, he stepped back until his whole body was pressed against the wall of the kitchen garden. He drew up his leg until it was at right angles to the wall, and then, with an almighty shout such as might have been heard before the walls of Jericho, he launched himself at the black door. God's strength will surely enter into me now, he muttered to himself a split second before he hit the door with the full force of the mighty, avenging ramrod of his own body.

When he opened up his eyes again, he found his poor body a broken, dishevelled heap on the doorstep. The door was now ajar. He peered wearily, dazedly, into the dimness of the hall – and there she was, staring back at him, mouth agape.

She stepped up to him, his very own Delphine, glorious in all her youthful beauty, and giggled behind her hand. He dropped his head in shame and waited for her chiding words. They were not slow in coming.

'If this is the best you can do, mister, it will not be good enough for the likes of him…' Those cruel words, so softly spoken, bit into him. He winced; but still he was burning like a furnace within. 'You are such a tender brute, mister, but still a brute, no matter how tender…' Her hand was upon his scalp now, like the body of some small, cold animal. 'Shall I teach you the words that you must speak in order to win me?'

He jerked up his head and met her eyes. He had expected reproach. None was there. Yet he must persist. He must not be duped by mere visions. Had not the good Lord whispered so much into his ear? He leapt up and thrust his dirty face at hers.

'You are a chimera, Delphine, and you have dragged along that first-born in your wake. I mean the one who is standing beside the window upstairs. That man spirited them here to defy me, and now they are in the grip of ghosts and demons. And though your father may be a man–' Well, he could not let her think he thought otherwise, could he? Otherwise, she would not have him – 'he too is a veritable demon... within. You will not stay my hand. I shall have them back again. Let me find them, Delphine!'

He lashed out at her with his hand, but before the hand could strike painfully against the door, she had withdrawn a pace or two as if by magic. He ran after her, further, further into the corridor of that house than he had ever in his whole life durst venture, but as he went to seize her about the waist, she thinned at the middle like an hour glass, leaving the top half to drift up the stairway and out through the long window of coloured glass on the turn of the stairs, smiling a tender, dissolving smile as she went, while the lower half seemed to sink through the floor at his feet...

What truth is there in this house? he asked himself, bewildered. Is even this door by which I entered not true then? He examined the side of the hand that had struck the door, and it was gashed and bleeding from the force of the blow.

God be praised, at least this door is true, he mumbled thankfully to himself, and then he kissed with no small passion the panel which was stained dark with his own blood, and even gave thanks for the fact that he could no longer flex the fingers of his damaged hand. Yes, they were still quite numb from the blow.

And as he let his eyes drift up that stairway again, he offered a small, quiet word of thanksgiving for the truth of his own body, and roundly cursed the devil for the evil one's power to conjure up the likeness of the woman he had once loved...

He pointed at the window through which the upper half of her body had vanished, and was intrigued to see that in so many respects it resembled the window of a simple country chapel such as the one down the lane in which they would all give thanks for his blessed Resurrection today, God willing. It was a tall, slender, round-headed window, and around its perimeter rectangular panels of coloured glass – violet, red, purple and blue – had been set.

As he ascended the stairway, his feet stepped into the bands of colour which the mid-morning sun had thrown down upon the steps. It is like a carpet, he thought; but there was no carpet beneath his feet, and the boards creaked unhappily.

He turned on the half-landing to face the second flight of stairs, and at the top he saw yet another long corridor stretching ahead of him. Its gloom depressed his spirits, and he wondered whether he should continue – for was it not more than possible that he was suffering from some sorry delusion? I have hardly slept, and my body has suffered so much torment, he thought to himself miserably. But he knew that he had not yet found his young charges, and that it was God's will that he should seek and seek again until he found...

And that I am determined to do, he said as he raised his leg to begin his ascent of that second flight of stairs.

But which of these two doors am I to choose? he asked himself when he had reached the middle of the corridor. One was to his left, the other to his right. The silence in the air was so heavy and oppressive, and the window and its parti-coloured sunlight so far behind him now that his very reason was made to grope again. He prepared himself to put his hand upon the first knob, but then thought better of it. Instead, he began to tiptoe along to the second door, but his feet felt so leaden that the best he could do was to slide them forward, inch by painful inch, or drag them along behind him as if they were some dumb, obdurate animals.

Who made these feet so heavy? he asked out loud, though in a whisper, but the only sound which drifted back in response to his question was the buzz of a small, circling housefly that proceeded to slap him upon the cheek, almost knocking him off balance, so shocked was he by that tiny assault upon his person. He hit out at it in all directions, flailing wildly, but soon grew so exhausted by his efforts that he desisted, and let the creature continue to land at whim upon leg, neck, arm.

'Which door then? Which?' he quizzed himself, fully concentrated once again upon the task in hand. I shall try the second, he thought, and, squeezing the knob boldly, he wrenched it to the left. He then pushed at it gently with his knee, and it opened inwards with barely a squeak. He thrust his head around the door.

To his surprise, there was little light within – merely a mild yellow glow, which made him marvel at the thickness of the curtains, that they should permit so little light to penetrate. At the far end of the room coals still burned in the grate, but even as he watched, that glow appeared to diminish in ardour. This fire has been neglected for an hour or more, he decided. The massive black mantle which overshadowed the fireplace was quite bereft of ornament. Above it there hung – o mockery! – a simple wooden crucifix. Otherwise the walls of the room were quite bare. And not a single piece of furniture was to be found in there either.

And yet it has not always been so, he concluded as he stared at the polished wooden floor, observing how it was scored with deep scratches, and how all those scratches seemed to converge on the door. They must have been in some teeming great hurry to remove it all then… Stepping across to the wall, he found further evidence of recent occupation. He saw that pictures – or hangings – had once graced these walls, for they were pitted with holes – the stigmata of nails driven crudely into plaster. And where they had hung, ghostly white patches – squares and ovals – had remained, yet more certain proof of human meddling.

He stood in the dead centre of that room and turned a full circle in order to assure himself that he had missed nothing. And as he did so, turning on his heel like a child, and gathering speed as he turned and turned until the walls began to whirl past and past him, he thought he heard the sounds of human voices through the wall.

He stopped then, reeling giddily, in order to listen all the more intently. The sounds increased in volume as he listened – from some distant, faint hubbub to a clear conversation, so clear that… yes… it *must* be true that they were on the other side of the wall, and he had chosen the wrong room. At the very moment that this realisation struck him, some person or persons began to rap on the connecting wall as if taunting him for his crass misjudgement. Without a second's hesitation, he stepped up to the offending wall and thundered upon it with his clenched fist.

'Do not presume, ye ungodly. I shall be with you in the blink of an eye!' And, having shouted these words of warning, he ran towards the door, skidding a little as he ran for that floor was highly polished. Flinging out his arm to steady himself, he jerked open the door.

He stood in the corridor, facing the door which led into the other room. Now I have them in my net, he thought grimly, lips so tightly pursed that they were bloodless. Without further ado, he wrenched the knob to the right and kicked back the door with his foot. He stood on the threshold, chest heaving, and took in the scene.

A large oak table, suffused with bright, joyous morning sunlight, filled the centre of the room. At the open window, the marmalade-yellow curtains flapped and danced freely in a balmy breeze. His eyes took in the disorderly remnants of a recent hearty breakfast – plates smeared with jam and buttery thumb prints; blackened fingers of toast which had left sooty marks here and there about the white table cloth. And on the floor, immediately in front of his feet, he saw a bread knife which had fallen from the table and been carelessly kicked aside. See how it spins upon its axis! he muttered to himself. And indeed it was still turning in a gentle circle, though now it had almost ceased revolving… But what of those people?

The clamour of human voices was still loud in his ears, but now, it seems, it was coming from beyond the window. Circling the table, and stooping to pick up the bread knife from the floor as he passed, he stepped up to the window sill and, resting his knuckles on the frame, leant out as far as he dared.

They were all moving in a crowd down the lane towards the chapel, children and adults alike. Although he could see them only from behind, he thought he recognised the principals: Madge, in the lead, furiously waving her arms about in the air; Lenny, who was leading young Jamie by the hand and giggling at his nonsense; and Dorin, who came up the rear, tottering on his legs.

But what incensed him so was the behaviour of the old man, who was leading Dorin by a stout rope, one end of which was attached, noose-like, to the boy's neck. And when the boy crawled to left or right to peer into the hedge or go after some pebble that he had thrown, he was caught smartly back by a sudden jerk of the old man's wrist and, as often as not, fell to his knees, which must, he guessed, be raw and bleeding now from all this hideous maltreatment.

'He shall not do such a thing to that lamb of God!' bellowed the man at the window, and, kneeling upon the sill, he leapt out with a most terrible cry to rescue them.

When he came to his senses again, he began to shake his head from side to side to ease the violent, thudding pain at his temples. Then, dragging himself to his knees, he crawled off in the direction of the chapel, sincerely believing that they were but a little way ahead of him.

To his dismay, the chapel door was shut fast

against him, and the sound of voices singing in unison reached his ears. 'So they have begun,' he grumbled, and retired to the shelter of a nearby hedge. He would wait for them to re-appear again. It would not be right to interrupt a service of homage to the risen Lord, though certain of those within may be in thrall to the wicked one...

His ears could not but be captivated by the sound of those voices singing 'Christ the Lord is Risen Today'. A shaft of sunlight seemed to illumine his darkened soul as he listened, and his worldly troubles were lifted from him in the same way that the heavy burden slipped from the shoulders of Pilgrim when his eyes first caught sight of the Cross of Calvary. He hummed along quietly to himself, and beat time upon the ground with his fist, imagining that he was conducting the massed choirs of the angelic host at the express wish of the Risen Lord. I am truly blessed to be chosen from amongst the multitude, he thought as he blinked and smiled into the sunlight. Then the singing stopped, and he heard the words of the itinerant preacher – did he not recognise the voice as that of Mr Henderson? – blessing them now and forever more. Now and forever more indeed, repeated the man in the hedge as he felt for the outline of the bread knife in his inside pocket. It was still safely stowed, thanks be to God.

The door of the chapel was thrown back by a short man of blotchy countenance whose thick, stubby fingers disgusted him. And yet he is God's creature also, the man reminded himself. Others streamed after him, talking idly about everything but the Lord's business: farmers' wives with great rolling thighs and elaborate hats of straw; thin, emaciated farm workers with vacant expressions upon their burnished faces. But it was not these that the man was waiting for, though he casually looked them over as they passed within a few feet of him. He counted up to twelve on his fingers, and still the ones whose appearance he was anticipating with such eagerness did not arrive.

When the general flow had ceased, the keeper of the keys – that overgrown boy – appeared at the door of the chapel, clasping the precious object to his bosom. He paused on the threshold and glanced up at the sky. As he gazed at the hurrying clouds, he jiggled the heavy key about in his hand, and whistled timidly, breathlessly the tune of 'Christ the Lord is Risen Today'. Perhaps this boy is contemplating the words of the sermon, the man thought, and he let him continue for a moment or two longer. Then, much to the man's astonishment, the boy suddenly reached behind him and jerked shut the chapel door. He thrust the key into the lock and turned it – twice.

The man picked his way out of the undergrowth with some care – after all, he did not wish to frighten the nervy creature – and stood waiting, a little back from him, staring. He could see a boil upon his neck, ripe for the lancing, which rubbed against the strangulating collar of his best Sunday shirt. The boy turned – and then jumped back when his eyes met those of the unexpected visitor.

'All locked up then,' said the man, pointing at the chapel door. The boy nodded. 'For how long though, boy?' The man tried to ease his mouth into a smile, but it remained an uneasy grimace.

'One whole week, mister, until I take up this key again…' They both stared down at the heavy old thing. 'The Sabbath comes but once a week, as the Good Lord ordained…' He cleared his throat and chipped at the earth with his toe. Evidently he was not a happy talker.

'There is something bothering me deeply, boy,' said the man, frowning at the top of the boy's head.

'What is that then, mister?' He blinked and cocked his head to one side. He did not know this queer man from Adam, and the smell of the Easter tea was already in his nostrils.

'The ones you have locked inside the Chapel.'

'Beg pardon, sir?' A look of extreme perplexity crossed his young face, which was already a rash of pimples. His brow furrowed, and he pushed a lock of lank ginger hair from off his sweaty forehead.

'I am concerned for those little children, locked up in this chapel with a sworn enemy of the Almighty God – and for a whole week together, it seems, if you will not free them.'

'What children are these, sir?' said the boy,

spreading his sparrow legs a little awkwardly.

'The ones that have lately been kept in the house with the black door. You know it well enough. It belongs to that tetchy old man you crossed this morning.'

The boy looked nervously about, twitching his lips like a rabbit, trying to frame a few words.

'You are mistaken, mister. They have all gone back, and the children with them. Even now they are eating their Easter tea – which is where I must go if you will pardon me…'

The boy made as if to take his leave, but as he turned away, the man's firm hand came to rest on his shoulder, and he stopped dead in his tracks. Now their faces were no more than a hand's breadth apart, which clearly did not much please the boy. He wriggled beneath the hand that held him, but not too much. He did not have the courage to do more – except with mere words.

'You must excuse me now for they are expecting me, and I am awful late already. There will be more trouble brewing if I do not return his key…' The voice was no steadier than it might have been. The boy made as if to go, but still the man blocked his path.

'And more trouble still, trouble heaped upon trouble, if you do not leave it with me, boy.'

A sudden panic gripped the boy. He let the key fall from his grasp and made a sudden dash for it. The man watched him go hell for leather up the lane. He glared after him, then stooped to pick up

the key of the chapel from the ground where it had
fallen.

As the hand which held the key moved
towards the lock, the man thought he heard the
sounds of those voices again inside the chapel,
which merely confirmed to him – if any
confirmation were really needed – just how foolish
or wicked – or both – the boy's behaviour had
been.

'They are all in league against me in these
parts,' the man said to himself, not at all surprised
by that discovery. Then he remembered how the
Lord had instructed his servants to be as cunning as
the fox and as slippery as the serpent when the
need arose. Such an occasion was without doubt
now upon him.

He pushed back the door and entered the
chapel. Being a rude and humble place of worship,
it was without a porch or any other encumbrance
which might have prevented his seeing the whole
interior at a glance, which consisted of a dozen
pews on either side of a narrow aisle, a plain
harmonium in the far corner, and a lofty pulpit
raised up eight feet or more above the ground.

Henderson's hands were resting lightly on the
edge of the pulpit, and when the preacher's eyes
met those of the man beside the door, he smiled
and beckoned him forward.

'Tread a little warily now, mister,' the man
muttered to himself as he walked slowly but

steadily up the aisle, 'be forever mindful of the devil's gins.'

'Look on his works, mister, for that is what you have come here seeking, is it not?' Henderson's voice boomed around that tiny chapel. With a flourish of the fat hand and a flap of the sleeve – he is still wearing that foolish cloak then, the man thought to himself – Henderson indicated the little group that was huddled in front of the pulpit.

'See how it has all been made ready, mister, for the time is short...' Henderson continued.

Yes indeed, now he could see them all clearly, a matter of feet away from him, squeezed up close together, and peering intently at a large table in front of the pulpit. They were all humming on the same note, making a single, continuous drone not unlike that of a swarm of somnolent bees, and when one of them abruptly ceased humming, his neighbour took up the strain, first a high voice, and then a lower...

And the old man was standing behind them all, arms draped across their shoulders, peering over their heads.

As the man stepped up, the group parted, some to the left, the others to the right, as if by some miracle. The Lord has parted the seas once again, the man mused lightheartedly, as that barber in Bodmin once deftly divided my father's hair down the middle... He smiled at this picture in his head.

And then, almost as if they had been warned of

his arrival, they all turned – and, to the left, now facing him, were ranged Jamie, Lenny and Delphine, and, to the right, Deg, Madge and Dorin. Not a single one of them is missing then, he thought, counting and re-counting his flock.

The old man, who had moved behind the others, turned also, and pressed his rough hands together in an attitude of prayer. His body blocked off all sight of the table. The man mocked him for that gesture of the hands, old pagan that he was, old, worm-eaten hypocrite...

Suddenly, the old man, who had been staring down at his hands, looked up. 'Your long journey is over, mister,' he said in an oozy, preacherly sort of way. There was a half-smile playing about his lips too. 'Won't you step up to enjoy the fruits of all your labours?'

He stood aside and indicated the box on the table. That Madge sniggered. Preacher Henderson, the nosy parker, was bent almost double over his lectern.

As the man approached ever more closely, he could not decide what sort of thing it was on the table. It had the shape of a small coffin, yet were those not wisps of straw that protruded from the edges? Could this be the first fruits of harvest time then? But how in the name of heaven could that be possible at this time of year?

But no, as he came up closer still, he saw it was indeed a small body that was lying so quietly in its box, eyes fully open. The fresh cheeks, ruddy as any early October apple, reminded him of his first-born; and yet was there not something suspicious about the colouring? He turned to the old man in anger.

'Who has waxed these cheeks?'

The old man stared back at him coldly.

'Ask yourself, mister. Ask the eyes.'

The man looked again, and indeed those staring eyes bore an uncanny resemblance to... 'This is the devil's work,' he shouted, 'to trick out a doll in this way!' And, snatching it from the box, he hurled it to the ground. Delphine screamed and threw herself upon him. They wrestled in a blind fury up and down that narrow aisle, and as he struck out wildly to left and right, some blows fanning the empty air, others connecting with the more tender parts of her body, he could hear the crowd noise swelling, urging first one and then the other on to a quick, decisive victory.

'These are such capricious, ignorant people,' he thought contemptuously, 'whose sole interest is in their cock-baiting.'

And then, with an almighty heave, he threw her aside, and her head struck the door of the caravan with a sickening thud.

'You have killed him, you have killed my first-born,' she whispered faintly before her body slumped to the ground, and he wondered if the others had heard. The crowd roared, and he acknowledged it briefly. 'And now let us all rest and pray,' he said, kneeling, and he held his eyes tight shut for the full count of ten. Then he, the victorious one, sprung to his feet to face the onlookers.

Six strange – though strangely familiar – anxious faces stared back at him.

'What have you been doing with my family?' he asked the old man with such savagery that his own children were obliged to wipe his spit from their faces.

'Whose family is that, mister?' asked Delphine tremulously from the floor, opening one eye. Just then, his attention was distracted by Henderson, who was pointing towards the door of the chapel.

'Your messenger is waiting, I think,' the preacher said coldly. That preacher never leaves off preaching, the man thought to himself disdainfully. Nevertheless, he turned to look in the direction of the pointing arm. The old man was standing in the doorway in his workaday clothes, rapping the key against his knuckles. Seeing the man staring back at him, he beckoned with his finger, a look of extreme exasperation upon his face. The man walked, meek as any chapelgoer, towards the open door. Better not incense him, he thought as he proceeded along a steady shaft of sunlight. It is not yet over by any means. Why – and here he chuckled to himself – we are not even proper wed yet...

'What exactly was it that you were seeking?' asked the old man when the other had drawn near. Only an inveterate liar would pretend to such ignorance, thought the other. All the same, he turned on his heel to point them out to him, thinking to please him by playing his silly little game. But they were gone. The chapel was quite empty.

The old man spoke again.

'All the children of this village are at their Easter tea, mister. And now I must lock up the chapel – with the *boy's* key, if you please…'

He handed it over – for what earthly use was it to him now? – and stepped out, somewhat dazed and heavy of heart – into the afternoon sunlight. As he trudged back up the hill towards the old man's house, he stroked his unshaven chin and wondered at their strange disappearance. His rheumy eyes brimmed with tears when he considered how they had once again slipped from his grasp. And he prayed as he walked, his legs moving ever more slowly as his words increased in intensity.

'Dearest Lord,' he prayed through a mist of tears, 'on this Easter Day, your servant has fallen victim to the most terrible delusions. He has been trapped, deceived, betrayed, by the most diabolical visions, and now he confesses not to know the difference between body and spirit. There in that stunted coffin lay the body of Deg, my first-born. And yet it could not have been he for it was a baby lying in straw that I saw, and a dead one at that. But that truth also was snatched away from me, for when I looked all the more intently, I saw that it was my own eyes into which I was gazing. And how can a man stare at himself, Lord, except in a mirror? And had it been a mirror, it would have shattered into a thousand fragments when I dashed it so impetuously to the ground. And yet I do not believe, Lord, that it was a human form at all. The cheeks were too waxy, the lips too ruddy, and the eyes too shiny. It was a marble I saw in those sockets, Lord, for the colours around the pupil seemed to swirl and turn as the colours in a child's marble are wont to do…'

And here he hesitated. His prayer had so confused him that he could not think how to continue. When he opened his eyes, that boy, that insolent keeper of the key, was standing just across the lane from him, leaning sloppily against a ramshackle gate, and chewing idly upon a wisp of straw.

'Where did you get that straw, boy?' snapped the man. His confidence had rushed back to him all of a sudden. The boy looked startled. What manner of man is this then? he seemed to be thinking.

'What straw is that you are speaking of, mister?' he replied, quickly thrusting himself upright and standing stiff to attention, stiff as that wisp of straw between his lips.

'The straw that your lips are fooling with, what else?'

The boy snatched the straw from between his lips, looked at it in astonishment, and threw it to the ground without further ado – almost as if the wisp had stung him.

'Why do you throw it aside now with such indecent haste? Tell me where you found it this minute or I shall kick your insolent head in!'

'It came from these parts, mister…' He pointed a trembling finger towards the hay loft that could be glimpsed beyond the gate.

'But what proof have you, boy?'

The boy said nothing. He glanced hastily to left and right. The lane was empty. The man came up very close, and emptied his next words straight into the boy's ear, not spilling a precious drop.

'Was it you that filled that box from the hay loft, boy, by any chance?'

'What box are you speaking of, mister?' The man cuffed him, once, twice – and thrice for good measure – across the cheeks for good measure; and the boy fell back, whimpering, against the gate. He raised a hand to his face – for whatever good that might do him. His eyes were big as a gooseberry with fright. Big as any gooseberry fool, thought the man.

'Lead me to that hay loft then. We shall soon see whether or not you are speaking the truth.'

He gripped the boy by the arm as they passed through the gate. Here at least is flesh and blood without a doubt, the man thought to himself sombrely as he fingered the boy's flesh.

They stood together in the entrance, and stared up at the bales of hay, heaped one on top of another to the height of ten or twelve feet or more in the corner.

'Let us go in now to see what can be found.'

The boy stood stock still. His whole body was quaking so much it seemed like the very ground beneath his feet was shuddering.

'But this is all there *is*, mister. What more do you expect?'

The man was surprised – and not a little displeased – by the boy's unexpected boldness of tongue. Still, he was not to be outfaced by some cud-chewer.

'It is no concern of yours what I expect, boy. We live by different masters, and yours I know from of old. Get in with you then.'

The boy, bewildered, uncomprehending, stumbled out of the sunlight and into the gloom of the hay loft. Then he turned, fearful of what might be expected of him next. The man stabbed at the far corner with his finger.

'Let us climb up yonder out of sight of the entrance way.'

The boy obeyed with great unwillingness. Indeed, he looked sick with dread, and he muttered a hasty prayer to God as he climbed. Now they were seated side by side on the topmost bale. The man gripped the boy's wrist again. Neither spoke for several seconds together. Then the man turned and stared deep into the boy's eyes. His heart was beating so fast and so hard that its movements caused his shirt to stir. His breath too was coming quick and shallow – like a breathless dog, all raging thirst, in the blistering sunlight.

'What do you call yourself then, boy?' the man asked him eventually. To the boy's astonishment, the eyes which had seemed to stare at him with such menace were now filmy, if not a little tender.

'My name is Tom, sir, Tom Trethewy,' he replied, hurrying out the words.

'And what name are you known by?'

'Beg pardon, mister?'

'By what name do your familiars know you?' said the man, looking all around him. There was enough hay in that loft to please a thousand cows – and plenty more to spare.

'Ginger, mister… on account of the hair,' he added, pulling at it as an afterthought.

'Do you talk to cats ever, boy?'

The boy dropped him a queerish look.

'What do you mean, mister?'

'Do you confide in cats when the others are paying you scant attention? That sort of thing…'

'Why no, mister. Never.'

'God be praised for that, Tom. They are just vermin – and let none tell you otherwise…' He nodded slowly and stroked the boy's back. It was a warm back – but his face was all coldness and suspicion still. 'You have sisters and brothers then?'

'I have had some, mister.'

The man's brow furrowed at the oddity of that remark. 'What exactly do you mean by that, boy?'

'There were the three of us, two boys and a

girl, Elsie…'

'And now there are…?'

'Two only, mister.'

'How so?'

'She drowned in the sea. My father lost her overboard from the boat last summer.'

The man's body stiffened at that news.

'And the body, boy? What of the body?'

The boy was some perplexed by that question.

'She just drowned in the sea, mister. There was no body.'

The man had never heard such a foolish reply to a plain, honest question.

'No *body*?' he snapped. 'There is always a body, boy. Do you not understand these things? If she had a body when living, she surely has one dead. What did your father do with the body of Elsie, boy? Tell me quickly.' He gripped him by the shoulders and began to shake him back and forth.

'Answer my question, boy. Are you too stupid to understand the words? Are they not plain enough for the likes of you?'

The boy burst into tears, and soon he was sobbing so hard that he could not speak whether he would or no. The man let go of him. He fell sideways onto the bale of hay and covered up his face with his hands.

For a while, the man seemed attentive to the boy's snuffles and sniffles. Then, all of a sudden, his own head slumped forward onto his chest and seemed to hang loose like a mannequin's. Now his eyes had a distant, vacant expression.

'It is a strange thing, burial at sea, boy. Your father will know that well enough if he disposed of the body.'

The boy looked at him with helpless, pleading eyes.

'But he did not do any such thing. He did not kill her or anything. He never found her at all...'

The man leant over him, his anger kindled afresh.

'How do you know such things? Were you in that boat too then?'

'N-no, my brother and I, we were swimming in the rock pool, out of harm's way...' The boy blinked as he spoke, stammering through his tears. He had such filthy streaks down his face from all that weeping and rubbing. 'It was a small boat, and he would not take more than one at a time, and she was chosen...'

The man looked pleased by what the boy had said.

'Yes, chosen, that is exactly the word. Death is a mercy at times, boy. Do not forget it. To release us from the snares of this world is a blessing – if you are at one with your Maker.' He lifted the boy's head from the hay by its hair and pressed their faces close together.

'Are you at peace with him, boy? Is your soul at rest? No lies this time, remember...'

The boy thought and thought, and all the while his eyes flittered about like minnows in a pool.

'Today I lost the key with which I am supposed to open the door of the chapel of a Sunday morning. The old man was exceedingly cross with me. I begged his forgiveness for my stupidity…'

'Anything else? Dig deep now…'

'…and I pray every day, morning and night, beside my bed.'

The man cupped the boy's face in his hand and smiled broadly.

'Then you are ready without the shadow of a doubt. Will you say a prayer with me now, boy?' The boy nodded. 'Do not speak the words out loud, mind. Only listen and mouth them after me. It is all that the Lord requires of you.'

The man pressed his palms together, having first arranged the boy's hands within his.

'Shut your eyes, boy, or you will not be heeded.' The boy did so. The man watched the boy's face to make sure that his eyes remained tight shut throughout the prayer. They flickered just a little – but never opened.

'Coming and going we are thine, Lord,' prayed the man. 'Even the dearest amongst us you clasp to your bosom for your own particular purpose. There is one here amongst us now who dwells in darkness; but, thanks to you and your manifold mercies, he will presently pass from darkness unto light. For this we thank you, most gracious Lord.'

He released the boy's hands gently. They remained pressed tightly together, pointing upwards, faithful, steady as a steeple. And, drawing from his inner pocket the bread knife, he drew it hastily, back and forth, across the boy's neck. Then he laid it aside, and, offering thanks for the sacrifice, washed his face in the welling blood, muttering over to himself 'His blood can make me whole' as he worked.

That done, he gathered the legs in his hands and pushed the knees up towards the boy's face. Up and up went those legs until the mass of him flipped back, head over heels, off the bale and, in falling, wedged into the space between the bales and the back wall of the loft – quite out of harm's way.

The man sat panting for a while, his chest heaving as he stared down at his hands. Now I am in no fit state for a Sunday tea, he told himself, as he eased his bulk down the mountain of hay.

Let me move with the utmost stealth, Lord, like a thief in the night, he prayed as he emerged into the light of day again. He crawled across the meadow on all fours towards that decrepit gate, and peered gingerly up and down the lane. Nothing but one lazy dog, he murmured, as he watched the sprawled creature panting in the sun.

Then, having girded up his loins, he raced past the chapel and down the lane towards the stream that crosses it before it disappears into the wood. And there he washed his hands and his face thoroughly, splashing the water everywhere, even behind the ears and down the back of the neck –

places which he seldom thought to visit these days.

That fresh, cooling stream water shocked him into a mood of strange clarity. He was seized with a sense of the urgency of his task. Soon day would decline to evening, and without a doubt the old man would lock his house fast against the onset of night.

Glimpsing a dark stain upon the left knee of his trousers, he knelt down in the stream again – it was shallow and pebbly where it crossed the lane – and agitated his leg in the water. Satisfied that the last vestiges of the blood had been quite washed away, he filled his mouth with water and flung his head about to soothe his parched throat, enjoying the sound that all that sluicing water made inside his mouth – like the slap of the sea against the sides of a wallowing boat. My words will come out all the cleaner for a gargle and a good spit, he thought to himself with some satisfaction.

His face was still tipped up dreamily towards the sky when the machine crashed into the backs of his legs with such a force that he was thrown forward into the stream. As he fell, he spread out his arms to save his face from the gravelly bed.

'Merciful God, what have we now?' he exclaimed as he writhed and spluttered in the water. Turning towards his assailant in a mix of bewilderment and fury, he saw a tiny child leaning across the handlebars of her red tricycle and eyeing him with great concern.

'I could not stop myself, mister. It just ran away with me, and I could not stop it...' she explained breathlessly.

Pushing the hair out of his eyes, the man smiled back at that small, tormented creature.

'Have you a name, girl?'

'Ellen,' it replied meekly, staring down at its naked feet which were now bent safely across the pedals, though now and again the toes squirmed a little around the rubber.

'That is a pretty name, child. Why are you not at your Easter tea with the others?'

She pouted prettily.

'They would not let me go.'

'Who is that, Ellen?'

'My father.'

'Where is he then?'

She pointed back up the lane, twisting her arm back behind her. But not once did her eyes leave the man's face. She is like an insect creeping across my skin, he thought, amused by her extreme curiosity.

'You are some lucky father's daughter, you know, Ellen.'

He reached out and enclosed her small, hot, puffy hand in his. She pulled it away quickly, wiping it, front and back, on her dress, and wrinkling her nose.

'Ugh, you are all nasty and wet.'

'And whose fault is that then?'

She did not reply. Slipping her thumb into her

mouth, she looked down at his arms, his legs, his feet.

'Do you swim?' she said. 'You cannot swim here, you know.'

The man shook his head sadly. 'I am no swimmer these days, Ellen. Swimming is not for the likes of old men like me.' He *had* swum though. He had been some swimmer in his time.

'I swim in the sea with my father. He holds me in his arms, like this—' She showed him how. '—and we swim together.'

'He is a good father to hold you tight and not drop you, Ellen.'

'I would not swim with you though…'

'Why so?'

'Because you do not swim. You would not know how to hold me. You might drop me.' The man nodded. She was a sharp one, this one.

'Have you ever seen your own face in the water, Ellen?'

She widened her eyes. They were greenish in colour. He thought he could see a small snake writhing inside them.

'No, but I have seen other strange things. Shall I tell you what they are?' She leant down towards him, and, cupping her hands around her mouth, whispered.

'Elephants!' He laughed out loud at that. She looked some cross that he had told the whole world her best secret. 'How many at one time, Ellen?'

'Only one because they are so big. You do not

see more than one. They never swim together.'

'And how exactly do they look?'

'That is a secret, my secret...'

'I can keep it.'

'Promise me that you will tell no other...' She wagged her finger at him. It was fat and red and stubby. '...especially that boy in the village who keeps the key to the chapel. He hits me with it when he catches me.'

'I shall keep your secret, Ellen. And you can be sure that I will not let that boy hurt you with his key again.'

'They look like...' She rolled her eyes around in her head.

'What then?' He was some impatient to know, for all that it was a silly child's game.

'Like – you! Because they are always blowing out water and rolling over and over in the wet!' She squealed with laughter at her own words. The man's mouth fell open. She saw his little black teeth.

'Surely that is whales you are thinking of, Ellen, not elephants. Whales are very dangerous creatures, you know. Have you heard tell of a man called Jonah?'

She spluttered into her fist.

'That is a woman's name, Joan. She is my mother.' She gave a little jump and clapped her hands above her head.

'No, Jonah I say! He is in the pages of God's holy book, the Bible. Did you not hear what happened to Jonah? Have they not told you in the Sunday School?'

She shook her head and looked very sad all of a sudden.

'I cannot go. He will not let me, my father. Nor to the Easter tea neither…'

What sort of father is this then? the man was thinking to himself. It is not just the old man who is gone in the head in these parts. So he told her instead.

'Jonah was eaten by a whale, but he did not die. Do you think, Ellen, that you would die if I ate you?' He went to grab at her – in jest or no, he could not quite tell – but she screamed, and, heaving at the handlebars of her red tricycle, pedalled back furiously up the lane.

The man sat on his haunches in the water and smiled at the tiny, retreating figure. She is ill served by that father, he thought to himself. Then, suddenly noticing how the clouds were chasing each other across the sky, he stood up in the water and shook the worst of it from him. And, retiring to the hedge, he dried his face and hands on a clump of grass and handsful of dock leaves.

This time I will behave less carelessly, he told himself, for he had no wish to be outwitted again. And he must by all means make haste now. They were surely all drinking and eating without him.

As he pulled his jacket closer about his person – the sun was fast sinking and the air cooling – he felt the outline of that knife in that inside pocket.

And when he withdrew it, he cursed, for it was still tainted.

The Entrance

He washed the knife blade scrupulously in the stream, running his fingers up and down its smooth, cool flatness, and peering at it closely for any last stray fleck of blood. When he was quite satisfied that all was well, he replaced it in his inner pocket and began to walk back up the lane towards the house again. He passed by that chapel on his left, wrapped in its own stillness, whose doorway was fast disappearing into the shadows of late afternoon. It is as well He draw a veil over that place, the man thought to himself, for it was there that I was so cruelly mocked by the Evil One.

Next he drew level with the broken gate on which that insolent keeper had been lounging and idly chewing his cud. God will not entrust such a one as that with the key to his heavenly kingdom, he pronounced grimly as he paused on his way to scowl.

His steps slowed as he drew near the house. The lane which ran between the front of the house and the kitchen garden was now chock full with vehicles of every description. He saw children's scooters thrown idly against the garden wall and, amongst several old motors, that old blue van of Henderson's which he recognised so well.

Out of simple curiosity, he stopped and peered through its side window. On the seat beside the driver's, he saw a large black Bible, its pages edged with gold. Two black silk bands – of the kind which separate one page from another – were hanging carelessly over the edge of the seat like the lock of some fine woman's hair. Only the very best will serve for the godless, the man thought contemptuously.

From underneath the Bible there peeped a fragment of pink ribbon which stirred his interest. He opened the door of the van and picked up the book. That ribbon too was marking some particular place in his Holy Word. The man let the book fall open across his palm, and lifted the fragment of ribbon into the air. How strange that it is not attached! he thought to himself. Upon closer examination, he became convinced that it was the very length of pink ribbon that Lenny always wore in her hair to keep it from falling forward into her eyes. And yet, surely, she would not have given it up so willingly… He quickly pocketed the ribbon, dropped the Bible back onto the seat, and slammed shut the door of that van.

He then turned his attention back to the house. He thought he could hear the skipping notes of a piano through the window of one of the lower rooms. Emboldened now, he positioned himself beside the garden wall immediately in front of that window. The curtains were drawn fully open, which pleased him greatly. Beside the piano there stood a girl of Madge's age and build – and general demeanour, and yet it was not quite her. Not quite.

In her hands she held a sheet from which she never took her eyes. Her legs were thin and white, her nose sharp and long. How beautiful are my own beside this gawky creature! he thought to himself as he listened to her sing.

It was a very displeasing song, the tune so harsh and jerky, and the delivery so shrill and uncertain that he winced, time and again, wishing that she would stop and give him back a little of his Sunday peace. But she did not. She was very determined to finish – as if, he thought, to spite me. The woman who accompanied her was no more pleasing to the eye. This one had short, stubby fingers with which she stabbed savagely at the keys. Each is trying to outdo the other, he thought. Suddenly, the woman pounded the keys once, with great violence, raised her hands up from the piano – and held them there like a child's pet begging for food. The girl glanced up, smiled, and quickly reddened. Her front teeth were strangely askew, and looked, in their regular alternation of white and black, a little like the piano keyboard itself. Then the pianist turned on her stool, causing it to squeak and groan beneath her great squashy bulk.

The man was greatly shocked by the sudden outburst of applause. It so reminded him of a tumultuous fall of rain that he even raised his hand to his head to reassure himself that no large drops had fallen upon it – for was not the sky above some terrible overcast now? Indeed it was. Having satisfied himself that his pate was as dry as any old bleached bone, he turned his attention back to what was happening inside that room. So absorbed had he been by the gawky girl and the fierce pianist that he had quite forgotten to examine the faces of those who had been listening with such concentration.

And there were so many of them, and all so rapt and eager, in that room to the left of the black door – surely too many by far for a room of that size… He scanned them all voraciously. Once or twice, a face he thought familiar looked his way, and the first time this happened, he dipped behind the wall. But when he raised his head again and found the face, it was still looking quizzically in his direction – at the height where his face would have been, he thought. Was that man looking behind him then, at another perhaps, who was watching *him* – just as he had watched the preacher when he was striving so impatiently to make the old man hear? But no, when he turned his head, there was no one there – or so it seemed.

Screwing up his courage, he raised himself up from the ground to his full height – but still there was no change in that man's facial expression. Then he noticed the white cane beside the man's chair, and he breathed a little more easily again. But only for a moment mind, for soon the man who was seated *beside* the gawper began to feel for the stick with his right hand, and as soon as he had found it, he gripped it firmly and began to rap steadily on the floor.

But it was not so much the adults he wished to

identify as the children who were seated cross-legged around the piano. There were some whose legs he could plainly see on the other side of the piano – the rest of their bodies were hidden from view – and these were the mischievous ones. One moment they would be sitting quite still, good as gold, and the next a heel would rise, and, shifting slowly to the left, fall like a stone upon the shin of a neighbour's leg; which caused both parties to shout and scuffle until the pianist, with some difficulty on account of her bulk, leant down and cuffed the two of them across the head. Could these be my ones? the man wondered to himself. They have never been of the gentle sort, in spite of all that schooling – and perhaps because of it. One thing at least was certain: the Easter tea was clearly over and done with. And, for the likes as such as these, a musical interlude was fit and proper.

Emboldened now by the fact that no one had shrunk back at the sight of his unfamiliar face rising above the wall, he stepped up to the door and rapped upon it with his knuckles. It was not a time for the mincing of words. The matter must be concluded once and for all. He waited a moment or two, and then began to drum upon the door with both his fists. His anger was rising like mercury up the tube. Then he began to shout at the door, believing in the power of his own breath to move mountains – and, in that case, what hope could there be for a mere door?

'Let me speak to the man of this house about

my children. He is holding them captive here, and I have come to rescue them. I am their father, and he is not within his rights to keep them from me!'

He waited and waited, and still there was no response. He tried the knob, rattling it about, but it would not turn. Could they not hear him shouting himself hoarse out there? Or was it that they – or rather he – simply did not *want* to hear? Could the old man be afraid, perhaps, of the wrath to come – afraid of the sheer, overwhelming force of his righteous anger? But why did not those little ones on the other side of the door come running to make themselves known to their dear father? It almost stopped his heart to ask that last question.

And then, as if by some miracle, he heard a voice speaking to him, and the sound of it seemed to come from the keyhole beside the door knob. He crouched down and put his ear to it. Now he would surely have some replies to his questions…

No sooner had his ear come level with the keyhole than a great jet of water was squirted into his ear drum. The blast struck him so forcibly that he was nearly toppled over. He shouted – more from the shock than the pain of it – and clapped his palm to the ringing ear. He rolled his head about to dislodge the water and ease the discomfort. And as he did so, he heard that same voice again… No, it was two voices now, one high and one low. They were laughing together and falling against the door, so overwhelmed were they by the success of their little joke.

If these rascals belong to me... he muttered, cursing them over and over again under his breath. Then he began to rattle the door knob furiously and pound upon it again with all his might until he was quite breathless with all the exertion. And *still* that door remained fast shut against him! He glared at it, spat upon it – and stamped back to his former spot in front of the window.

The scene was so changed now that he first checked to assure himself that he had not mistaken one window for another. He stepped across to peer through the downstairs window on the other side of the porch, but here the curtains were drawn against the light, and all seemed utterly still within. Had that been so an hour ago when he had first marched up, dripping, from the stream? For the life of him, he could not precisely remember.

The rain came on at last, heavy, spasmodic drops in the beginning, but it little bothered him now. Who could be wetter than I, Lord? he prayed, shrugging, as he raised his head skyward. Then he returned to his former spot in front of the window, and again scrutinised the interior of that room where they had been so busy with their musical interlude.

A man, no more than forty years at a guess, was now reclining on a chaise-longue which seemed to fill the entire window space. That is a bone-idle face, the man thought angrily. The young man's hands were crossed over the buttons of his waistcoat, and his thumbs were beating time to the music. Slowly, lazily, he yawned a great, open-mouthed yawn, but he did not trouble to cover up his mouth, and the yawn continued for several seconds.

Who is this idle fellow? thought the man on the wrong side of the window, for he did seem, in part at least, to recognise the lineaments of the face. And yet, at the same time, he did not... Suddenly, the younger man raised his left hand and began to tap with the nail of his index finger upon the window pane. That is the clean finger of one unfamiliar with toil, the man thought contemptuously. When the nail had first struck against the pane, he had thought that the idler might be beckoning him inside – but no, he was not even watching his own finger; and it was moving to the same rhythm as the thumb of the hand that still idled on the waistcoat...

The man turned his attentions to the piano. It is without a doubt the very same piano, he assured himself. But was it standing on that spot last time? He thought not. Nor was he gazing any longer at the profile of that portly pianist. Now it was the back of a much younger woman, much younger and more comely altogether which met his eye. Even from the back he could see how much that lovely creature was exerting herself. Yet it was never quite good enough, it seemed, for the idler in the waistcoat. Often she would stop and let her hands fall wearily to her sides. Then the man would turn his face towards her, utter some doubtless uncaring word or other, and her hands would rise slowly and obediently to the keyboard again. The tune which she was practising with such determination was known to the man outside the window – but he could not quite give it a name. In which case, it cannot be a hymn, he thought. Profane music then…

That this man should teach her such things! He frowned angrily at that soft, contemptuous face, but the young man's only response was to shrug off one of his slippers and flex his toes. The man marvelled at the grey worsted stocking that was exposed to view – that they could afford such luxuries in these parts!

On and on she practised, now flagging, now returning to the keyboard. It seemed that it would never end, this terrible music lesson. When will he release her? the man wondered, still gazing with pity at that young, comely back as the rain streamed down the back of his neck.

Suddenly, she snatched the music from its stand and flung it at the idler. It hit him full in the stomach. The man outside clapped his hands and did a little dance for joy. She has some spirit, this one! he thought. Then, slamming down the lid of the piano – how the window rattled when she did that! – she let her head fall forwards on to her folded arms, and her whole body began to shake violently.

His heart went out to her. See what this teacher

of piano – if that is what he calls himself – has achieved with his tyrannical ways! he said to himself, shaking his head dolefully from side to side. His eyes brimmed with tears. Then the young man in the room opened his mouth, and angry words poured forth, words which, to the man watching from outside, seemed to resemble utterances in a dream.

'To your room, Delphine, for you have disobeyed me!'

She raised her head and turned her pitiful face towards him.

'I shall not go, father. You will have to kill me first!' Her face fell forward again, and she began to wail and sob out loud. He swung his legs down from the chaise longue and walked swiftly across to her.

It shall not come to pass, thought the man. Merciful God, do not let it happen! She is mine, this one. He will not hurt her, that tyrant of a father. And, heaving the topmost stone from the wall against which his whole body was straining, he pitched it with all his might at the window.

'I will wreak such havoc that none shall withstand me!' he shouted aloud in defiance, and promptly ran round to the door again.

Now it was open – but barely more than a fraction. And though his body had been full to the brim with anger and pent up rage, he now hesitated on the threshold because he had not expected to gain such easy entry. Curb yourself a little now, he whispered, anticipating some trick. He pushed gingerly at the door with his foot, and it swung open, fully open…

Young Lenny was standing before him in the hall. She smiled when she saw who had arrived and approached him boldly. 'Our father,' she said, taking his hand. She tried to lead him inside with her, but he stood firm on the threshold, nursing his suspicions.

'Wait, Lenny,' he whispered. 'Tell me first who exactly is in this house with you.' She laughed lightly and screwed up her face.

'What a funny question you ask me, father. Why, there is Madge and Dorin and Jamie…'

'And what of Deg? Where is that Deg? Is he not here also?'

She looked up him again, but now she was no longer smiling.

'Do you not know what has happened to him, father?'

'If I knew, I would not ask you, would I, Lenny? Is your father one to ask a foolish question?'

Hurt by that reproach, she hung her head in shame and said nothing. He tapped her gently on the shoulder, and when she still did not respond, he thrust his hands beneath her armpits and lifted her up into his arms. Still she would not speak to him. She buried her face deep in his shoulder. He felt her teeth gnawing at his jacket. He pushed his hand beneath her chin and gently levered up her head until their faces met. Still her eyes remained fast shut. She is willing them shut, he thought, reining in his anger. He tickled her chin with his finger.

'Who is the very best reader in our household, Lenny?' he whispered into her ear.

'I do not read now. I do not know how to,' she said through her clenched teeth without opening her eyes.

'You cannot read, Lenny! What sort of a joke is that? Who will read that Bible to us around the table of an evening if Lenny, our best reader, cannot read any more?'

'Let the Tittle-Tattler do it, father.' Was she taunting him?

'You know I have no time for that teacher, Lenny, and you will not speak her name in front of me.'

She scowled and snorted down her nostrils. He blew upon the lids of her eyes, but still he could not coax them open. Here is a stubborn creature, he said to himself. And yet he would not force her against her will. She had too much to tell him.

'You say that your brother Deg has been here with you today then?' he asked her as if they had been talking quite happily to each other about this, that and the other.

'No, that I did not say, father.' Now she opened her eyes – and quite shocked him with her fixed stare.

'What did you say then, girl? And be not too

long about it for I must also talk to your sister and brothers.'

'He is in this house, father, but he says he will not speak to you.'

Impatient with this girl and her strange replies, he let her slip to the ground, and straightaway she ran off into the house. And as she disappeared into the room which held the girl and the piano, she turned and cocked a snook at him.

Loitering in that dim passageway for the second time that day, he wondered at the news that Deg had returned to them. Could it really be true after all? And what did she mean when she said that the boy would not speak to him? And could it really have been Deg that he heard this morning when he crouched behind the wall of the kitchen garden, listening to that high, clear note above all that clamour of voices? But how? How?

Suddenly, the door to the back kitchen opened and the old man appeared, looking awful sullen beneath the neb of his cap. Almost without thinking, he pressed his body as close to the wall as possible. The old man stopped in front of him and eyed him coldly.

'What manner of man or beast is this that slinks away in some corner?' The old man spoke so harshly that he could not find the words with which to reply to his question. 'You want her, you say,' the old man went on, 'and yet you do not want her. I put my boot upon your shoulder, mister, and you do not even raise your pretty young head to look me in the eye – me, me, a man old enough to be your father, and you a young and virile trapper of rabbits, or so she tells me when I can squeeze the least word out of her… Not that she is to be believed for one single moment, being her mother's daughter and not an idea in that flighty little head of hers. Too stupid, I reckon, even to be loved and courted by the likes of some lowly rabbit trapper. What do you say to all these things? Or have you not words enough in your brain to answer an honest man's questions?'

The rabbit trapper swallowed and fingered his stubble nervously. I cannot see his eyes for the neb of that cap, he thought. Perhaps that is all to the good.

'*Still* no words?' continued the old man sarcastically. 'I can see that you are a man who takes an insult lightly, one that turns the other cheek. Isn't that what they say of the likes of you?'

The old man's breath smelt sour and threatening. Be gone from me, Satan, said the trapper, over and over to himself as he listened.

'Very well suited then, I think, mister, for they do say that one weak sapling will support another if the wind does not trouble to uproot them, don't they now? Would you call yourself a sapling – or not?'

And still he could not find the courage within himself to reply to the old man's taunts.

'There is one more question still, and this time

I would be so grateful if that tongue inside your head could flap about a little. They do say you speak in tongues, don't they?' He grinned mockingly.

Now he blasphemes, the other thought impotently.

'Give me a sight of those muscles in your arms, mister,' the old man whispered into his ear.

Obediently, the man threw off his jacket, which slapped against the floor of the hall. He stared after it as if it were an abandoned friend. And very soon those empty sleeves will be oozing water, he thought. He rolled up his sleeves in great haste and held his naked arms stretched out in front of him.

'Now crook them a little...' said the old man. He did so. The old man flicked at the biceps with his finger. First he tittered; and then he began to laugh uncontrollably, clutching his stomach within his folded arms, practically bent in half by the time he was done. After a decent interval, the trapper rolled down the sleeves of his shirt and stared blankly and pitifully ahead of him.

'Your strength is wholly of the spirit then,' continued the other. 'That you would surely not deny – or would you?'

'God is indeed my strength and stay,' he muttered at last, though still half under his breath, 'and no word of mere man can touch me.'

The old man smiled, pleased that he had at last provoked him into speech. He raised one finger in the air.

'Answer me this one question then now that you seem to have found the tongue that lodges in your head. Would you not say that your frame was too feeble by far to bear such a burden as the one with which I saw you stumbling down that cliff path?'

'And yet God gave me the strength to bear it, that cannot be denied,' replied the trapper.

'And what exactly was in that bundle with which you were struggling with such difficulty on that morning?'

The trapper averted his gaze. Just then, he saw a tiny bantam hen on the threshold, its head cocked to catch his every word – or so it seemed to him just then.

'It is a private matter between myself and my God,' he replied, the words running swiftly out of his mouth. 'I cannot give you any other answer.'

The old man sniffed.

'I think that you are withholding something from me, mister. Of course, I would not want to force an answer out of you. After all, you are a reasonable man. But a secret – any secret – can prove a stumbling block between a man and his maker, can't it?'

'My innermost thoughts are known to my maker. Nothing is concealed from Him.' He spoke the words loudly, the better to convince both parties. Yet still the old man wheedled.

'But if there *is* something shameful which you dare not confess to another man – not even to the preacher, Mr Henderson, for example – should that not be a matter of some concern to you? What if – after all – you were an instrument of the devil?'

At last the trapper's confidence returned to him. What devil was this to call him devil? He wagged his finger in the old man's face.

'If you are going to talk to me in this way, I would be happy to dispute with you which is the greater devil of the two of us. Are you not holding my children captive in this house?'

The old man laughed and opened his arms.

'How can *that* be? My door is always open. See for yourself. Inspect the evidence for the truth of my words. Look behind you…'

He looked. The door was indeed still ajar, though the bantam had skipped off. In its place, he saw Dorin, his very own Dorin, playing happily upon the step. He stepped out to greet his son. If there are two, they must all be here, he thought, a little lighter of heart. He was just about to clasp the boy to his bosom when the old man's voice rang out behind him.

'You seem to have forgotten that I have something to show you. Mr Henderson himself will vouch for the truth of what I have to say.'

He turned, perplexed by these words. Henderson was standing behind him, leaning over the old man's shoulder with a look of stern admonishment upon his face. That is just the way he leans down from the pulpit, the man thought, edging back a little. The old man raised his arm, offering his open palm for examination.

'See what I have here in the palm of my hand,' he said. It was a fine white powder. The old man was stirring at it with his index finger. The trapper stared at that small, white hillock, and the more he stared, the more his body began to shake uncontrollably.

'What is it then, mister?'

The old man was waiting for an answer, but the other stepped back.

'I do not know,' he replied, wiping his brow with the back of his hand.

Just then Henderson, coming out from behind the old man, whispered a word or two into the trapper's ear. 'Are you not familiar with the words of the Holy Book, mister? Does it not say somewhere "Let them eat sherbet" — as the good Dorin is now doing...?

The man wheeled round to see Dorin, his very own Dorin, licking the white powder off his palm. First he would suck at the end of his finger, wetting it thoroughly; then he would dip it into the powder and pop the whitened finger end into his mouth...

'Why do you mock me so, you two?' shouted the trapper, turning back to see the grins on the faces of the old man and the preacher. 'Is God so wholly absent from your lives that you are driven to torment me in this way?'

They laughed together at his words. Then the old man raised the palm of his hand until it was on a level with his mouth, and Henderson, darting his head forward, blew the powder full into the trapper's face. Coughing and spluttering, he reeled back, rubbing his eyes and cursing. He began to kick out in their direction, screaming for all he was worth.

But by the time he was able to see again, the two had disappeared. They were so afraid of my wrath that they were forced to flee, he told himself with some satisfaction.

No sooner had his sight been restored to him than he heard a most violent scuffle behind the door of that music room. All of a sudden, it was flung back, and the girl flew out, her hair streaming behind her. They collided with such force that their bodies collapsed in a heap on the floor.

'Help me, oh help me,' she whimpered, burying her face in his shirt. The father followed soon after, still lacking the slipper he had thrown off earlier. He stood over them, eyes ablaze with anger and contempt.

'Stand up this minute and face me, Delphine,' he commanded. 'Do not seek solace in the bosom of some filthy tramp.' He grabbed her by the hair, but the trapper clung to the sobbing girl – and she to him for she was fearful of the force of her father's arm.

'Do not maltreat this girl. She has done you no wrong. See how afraid she is of your strength. Are you not ashamed to frighten her so?'

The girl and the trapper looked up into the face of the father. Now he was hesitating a little.

He had not expected such bold, clear words from the mouth of one so seeming lowly.

'What do you call yourself, mister?'

'I live hereabouts, and my business is the trapping of rabbits,' he replied with artful coyness, exasperating the man.

'Can you not answer my question? Is there no particular name by which you are known?'

The trapper smiled up at him from the floor for asking so naive a question. He even puffed himself up a little to impress the girl.

'My name is nosed abroad already in the courts of heaven. In fact, it is written in the Book of Life by the hand of the Almighty himself. What more do you require of me?'

Hearing that, the younger man fell to his knees and begged his pardon. The rabbit trapper placed his hand upon the head of the kneeling man, and spoke these few words into his ear: 'I have nowhere to lay my head, and my sole glory upon this earth is my children, who have been rudely snatched away from me. She who bore me these children sits even now astride my chest, seeking solace there – and it is entirely fit and proper for a wife so to do...'

He lay there smiling to himself, wrapped about in a pleasurable mist, the kneeling supplicant quite forgotten. Her weight is resting comfortably upon me, he was thinking. Then he drew her face down to his and squeezed it. How many long days is it, he asked himself, since I have known such human comfort?

Quite soon he began to shiver from top to toe. After all, he had fallen upon his jacket, which still retained much water. His teeth began to chatter uncontrollably inside his head, and he was forced to clench his jaws to stop them.

When he looked up at her again, it was the face of Madge, half in shadow now, that was staring back at him. He sat up with a sudden jerk, which pitched her off him and onto the hard stone flags. She cried out, rubbing her hip.

'So I've found you at last, young Madge,' he snapped. 'You are a weasel, girl. What did you mean when you wrote in that letter of yours that you had gone with him because I could no longer nourish and protect you? What nonsense was that? Do you not know he is my sworn enemy? Did I give you permission to dance to his tunes?'

At each new question, he stabbed her in the chest with his finger end. She winced at every stab. 'Speak to me now, girl. Make your intentions known to me. Will you destroy this loving family of ours?' She stared and stared at the ground. Her features seemed set in stone. And still he persisted. 'How many times have you slipped away to tell him all that I have said and done? How many times have you betrayed me? And what do you know about the visit of Deg to this house? Have you indeed seen that boy with your own eyes?'

The more questions he threw at her, the less inclined she seemed to answer. And when he began to speak of her beloved Deg, she turned her face to the wall and scratched at the plaster with her finger. The white flecks began to fall like snow into her lap. And as she worked and worked at her scratching, she hummed some teasing little melody underneath her breath which she made up as she went along. Or so it seemed to the father who watched her, his face reddening with outrage when he saw what scant attention she was paying him. At last he stopped talking. There was nothing more to be said. He had rung himself dry.

Now she turned to him, bold as brass. She grinned mischievously and, putting out her hand, tried to close his eyelids with her fingers. He flicked his head from side to side as if trying to rid himself of the attentions of some bothersome insect.

'Away with you, you tormenting girl! What do you think you are doing to your father's face?'

'I was just seeing whether your eyes would close when I put my fingers upon your eyelids, and of what stuff they were made, those all-seeing eyes of my father…'

'What nonsense is that you are talking, girl? These eyes of mine are always open, alert and sharp to needle out truth and falsehood. Would they be otherwise?'

She looked at him somewhat askance as if he had said something most peculiar.

'You can close your own eyes when you want to, father – yet you could not close our mother's. Why could you not do such a tiny miracle as that for your own children? Then we would have followed you to the ends of the earth, and not deserted our dear father for another…'

He simply could not believe that such mysterious and confused words were pouring from the mouth of one so young. He stared back at her, speechless. She tittered a little – then stopped herself with a bunched fist. He laid his shaking hand upon her forehead.

'Are you well, my Madge? You are not feverish or anything, are you, to be saying such things to the father who has always loved and protected you?'

Her face crumpled like paper in a blaze, and tears began to flow. So fire and water do mix if the conditions are ripe, he was thinking to himself.

'What ever is the matter now, girl?' he said, shaking her a little too roughly.

'Our father, I am terribly upset that you have returned to us in this way, full of your anxious questions, and with those great, watery eyes of yours popping out of your bruised, old face. If I could choose…' she paused, stroking the flesh of his cheek with her finger, '…if I could only have chosen, I would not have had such a father as you, father. It is all true what you say. We abandoned you for another. We were sore frightened in that caravan, all huddled up together at nights, crying in that corner furthest from the door through which we had bundled our mother. And we followed him because he spoke to us of our Deg; where he was, and on what day he would return to us. And he *has* returned, father…'

There she stopped. She turned her face to the wall again and said no more. He drew her body to his. Now it was wholly limp and compliant. He laid her across his shoulder and gently patted and stroked her back. She felt like some child's old rag doll in need of winding, those eternal comforters…

'There, there, my Madge,' he murmured, 'you need fear him no longer. I am come back to you, and between us we shall solve the mystery of Deg about which he has spoken, that treacherous man…'

Her body suddenly stiffened at these words. She drew her head back over his shoulder and looked into his face. Her eyes were clear and bead-bright – yet puzzled.

'There is no mystery, father. He is with us today as the man promised he would be. Did you not hear him speak this morning?' She sighed and shook her head. 'How wonderful it was… And when our mother returns to us also, all will be as before – as you so solemnly promised us on that day…'

'Where is my Deg then?' he asked cautiously.

'You mean you do not know, father?' She scrambled to her feet and clapped her hands. How lively she now seems! he thought, smiling at her teasing words.

'If I knew, I would not ask you, Madge.'

She pointed up the stairs, one quick, darting stab.

'He is above us, father, in that upstairs room.

Will you not come and speak to him?'

'That I will certainly do if it is as you say, our Madge.'

He dragged himself to his feet, and turned to face the stairs up which she was already scurrying. On the turn of the stair, he saw her reach up to take her mother's hand. He nodded contentedly, knowing for certain it was the hand of Delphine. I would recognise the least little particle of my beloved, he told himself, smiling. Then he felt around in his pocket for his snuff box. That stream must have had it, he decided after a few moments of fruitless searching within the lining of his jacket. How little is needed to reduce a man to a state of extreme melancholy, he reflected.

And how witless of a man to be discomfited by such trivialities! he continued, cheering himself just a little.

The Upstairs Room

So I am ascending these stairs for the second time today, he mused as he watched his feet feeling for each new step. And this time shall be my last, and the mystery will be concluded, he added in hope, impatient to be done with it all.

The head of Dorin was nudging against the backs of his legs as he climbed. Grasping the rail of the banister to steady himself, he lashed out backwards with his foot, sending the boy tumbling down the stairs again.

'Do not hinder me upon my mission, boy,' he shouted angrily, tossing the words back over his shoulder. 'It is a critical hour this one, and my strength is nearly spent. Get back to your childish games in the porch.'

He reached the half-landing, and there he paused, hands on hips, wheezing heavily. Through the long window which so reminded him of a chapel's, he could see the lane which wound down hill – past the gate and the chapel – to the stream. A small crowd was milling there, bodies weaving in and out of each other, their talk so confused together that to his ears it resembled the low drone of insects. And the humans themselves reminded him of termites moving in a slow, undulating mass upon a heap of dung, ever shifting and turning and climbing, but the whole swaying clot of them staying put upon one spot in spite of all that ceaseless motion.

Such a sight dismayed him, and he spat upon the window as if by spitting he would cleanse himself of this vision that so disgusted him. But when he looked again – and he could not, for all his disgust at the sight that met his eyes, quite resist looking – it seemed to him that they were bearing a box upon their heads. And this box was pitching and tossing so wildly that he grew afraid it would fall between them to the ground, spilling out its contents.

'The trouble with these people is that not a single one of them can bear to take the burden upon himself... No sooner does the box touch someone's outstretched arms than he pushes it away from him as if fearful of contamination. But if that is indeed so, why do they not disown it? Why do they not toss it aside and go their separate ways? The answer, of course, is that they cannot. They must continue to bear its weight for their sins – that is as plain as day – though not a single one of them can bear to touch it for a moment longer than is absolutely necessary...'

As he mused out loud upon the strange behaviour of this shifting human mass, he saw that he had been deceived – on one point at least. It was not, as he had first thought, rooted to the spot at all...

Little by little, it had been flowing up the lane;

and, indeed, the leaders had now seized hold of the garden gate, and were beginning to push it open… He scoffed at their torpor, and mocked them for the fact that they were not able to act in haste to achieve their ends. And yet, in spite of his taunts, he soon became utterly convinced that by the day's end the whole seething mass of them – together with that pitching box – would be at the door of the house, if not inside…

He screwed his knuckles into his eyes, welcoming the pain and the darkness that ensued. Now that my eyes are free, God will surely assist me to turn my body, he mumbled. And he screwed his body around in a full circle so that it was now facing up the second, shorter flight of stairs. Who would have guessed that to turn a body such as mine would require an effort equal to that of twisting a screw into an oak with one's bare hands? he marvelled. He stared anxiously down upon his hands, flexing the fingers. And then, remembering that he had nevertheless achieved this seemingly impossible feat, he clapped them together, and the scene quite vanished from his head.

He ascended briskly the second flight of stairs, humming as he went and drumming his fingers upon the banisters. Again he considered the problem of the two doors. In which room will I find that elusive first-born? he asked himself jocularly. That Madge is bound to be up to her little tricks again, and it is perhaps a father's lot –

sometimes a happy one, sometimes not – to pander to a child's whims…

He tapped upon the door of the room which had been bare earlier in the day. It opened without hesitation – and, sure enough, the face of Madge appeared, bright, pert, and as if quite prepared for his arrival. She smiled briskly and spoke a few words to him. The noise of merriment coming from within was so great that he could not quite catch what she said. He bent forward, leaning on his knees, and, raising his voice, asked her to please repeat what she had said to him because that infernal racket had made it quite impossible for him to hear her words.

'We are all celebrating the safe return of our brother and our mother,' she shouted into his ear.

He nodded, and asked tentatively whether he might not join them in the room. She put her finger to her lips, pointed to someone behind her that he could not see, stepped back, and promptly closed the door, nearly trapping his fingers as she did so. He blew upon his finger ends, nursing the imagined injury, and frowned at the door, a little hurt by the way she had treated him. Surely they are all waiting for me, he said indignantly to the door. The door, being nothing but door, looked blank and uncomprehending.

Suddenly, he heard the noise of many feet upon the lower stairs. He ran to the banisters and leant over. They had arrived already! Seven or eight of them were squeezing up the stairs, each trying to outdo the other. They were panting heavily, cursing one another, and flailing out wildly with their fists. He saw a stricken one fall with a single, plaintive cry. As the body slid between them, bumping backwards down the stairs, he saw one land a well-aimed kick to its temple. The body went quite limp, and promptly disappeared from view. The box was still rocking back and forth across their heads.

The one at the front looked up and saw him leaning down and staring hard at them.

'Are you ready to take the delivery, mister?'

'What is it that you bring? I am not the man of this household...'

Then the voice of the old man boomed out all of a sudden from below.

'This is the place. Have no fear. He was not to know of its arrival. That one has enough with his own dark secrets.' The crowd guffawed at that. Am I known to them then? the man asked himself.

Suddenly, he heard the door to that room at his back opening again, and he quickly stepped up. I must not miss my opportunity, he thought. Madge slipped out sideways and closed it carefully after her.

'Are you ready for me then, daughter?' he asked cautiously, for he regarded her as the keeper of the door, and one, therefore, to be won over with quiet blandishments. She looked up into his face, then down at his person. All was not well. He could see that from the strange upwards twist of her mouth.

'It would be foolish of me to ask you to cleanse yourself, wouldn't it, father?' Her words shocked him.

'Does my appearance disgust you then?'

She put on a look which seemed to say: I must be patient with this thing. After all, a thing is but a thing...

'I know you for what you are, father, but there are some inside who might regard you as a stranger in your present pitiful state.'

He scoffed at her words. He? A stranger? Could there be a man less strange than he to his own family?

'You are playing with me, Madge. It is not possible that my dear ones will fail to recognise me. It is not so long since I saw them...'

'I grant you it is not a long time as days upon this earth are measured, father, but in other ways...'

At that he grew a little impatient with her tomfoolery.

'What ways are you speaking of, girl? See this hand...' He thrust it in front of her face. 'Is this not the hand that has always protected and defended you and your kind?'

She pinched a finger end between her thumb and forefinger, then quickly let it drop again.

'As I say, father, it is not I you must convince. It is the others...' She began to turn away from him.

'Well, let me talk to them then. Let them

examine for themselves this old body of mine and see just how familiar it is.' He grinned at her through the odd tooth that still remained in his head. 'Surely they have not forgotten me so soon...'

There was a look of sorrow in her eyes now. Was it real or feigned?

'We do not speak of you any more, you know.'

'Why so, our Madge?' His voice came out loud and hearty.

'We believed you to be dead, father. How could a man as ancient as you survive in such conditions?'

Was she teasing him?

'Let me present them with the evidence of myself then! We shall find out soon enough which one of us is speaking the truth.'

'As you wish, father, but do not get upset if I ignore you in there.'

What incredible words were these? Was this not flesh of his flesh that was speaking?

She put a finger to her lips and drummed upon them, thinking.

'Nothing is decided, father. All is yet to come,' she replied, heaping enigma upon enigma as she threw open the door and presented him to the assembled company.

How closely it resembles my imaginings! he marvelled as he watched the children dancing frenziedly in a ring about their elder brother. His swarthy arms were raised high in the air, and he had eyes for none but these young ones who shrieked and jumped in his shadow. The man in the doorway swelled with pride that he should have borne such a manly boy, and he stepped forward, hand outstretched in welcome.

Lenny was the first to speak.

'Do not break our magic circle, old man!' she shouted out breathlessly as she danced. 'You must not touch our loving brother, for he has only now returned to us from Redruth, and he must go back whence he came within the hour.'

Shocked to be so rebuffed, the man turned to seek out Madge, but she had left his side. Now she was kneeling in the corner at the bedside of her mother. Creeping around the perimeter of that whirling, shrieking circle of dancers, he tiptoed up to the bed. *Perhaps it will be best if I do not make myself known to the brother until I have made my peace with Madge and our mother,* he was thinking to himself. And so he approached them, like a thief in the night, head averted…

When he had reached the bottom of the bed, he fell to his knees and curled himself up like a docile cat, ears pricked open for the conversation at the head. Out of the corner of his eye, he could see a length of trailing bandage. *It is still in its place then,* he thought, marvelling at his own dexterity. *She will not catch her death while that bandage gives her a little warmth and comfort.*

Suddenly, the bed began to shake and tremble.

The man's head jerked up — he could not help himself, so shocked was he by that unexpected violence. Young Jamie had broken away from the circle of dancers, and now he was bouncing up and down on that groaning mattress, shrieking and laughing. And as he danced, Delphine shot out an arm to tickle or to prod at him, which made him leap about all the more frenziedly. Then, in order to trick the child, she let her head fall back on the pillow like a stone and feigned sleep — except that her eyes remained open. Jamie, wise to these antics, crept further up the bed still and, giggling to himself, peered deep into her eyes, and waited for her to surprise him all over again....

The boy was poised in this way directly above his mother's face when suddenly — who knows why? — he turned his head and met the eyes of his watching father. A look of mingled fear and distaste pulled his young features awry, and, slowly but surely, he climbed down from the bed, holding his father's gaze all the while, and, with a final breathless scamper, disappeared beneath it. The man peered after him, but all was pitch dark under there and nothing stirred. Twice he spoke the name of his youngest son into that dusty murk, but all remained utterly still. Let him bide his time then, the little scamp, thought the man. Let us see how much joy the darkness will hold for him by and by...

Raising his head above the bed once again, he stared hard into the face of his wife. She was still feigning sleep – head upon the pillow, mouth agape, eyes wide as saucers. Perhaps she is waiting for me to do as Jamie did so that she can surprise me too, he thought to himself. In which case, let me do it then – it is a pleasurable enough little game...

But no sooner had he rested his knee upon the bottom of the bed than the dancing stopped and a deep silence descended upon the room. The man withdrew his leg in all haste and turned awkwardly to face his eldest son, who was glowering at him from the centre of the circle, arms crossed upon his chest. The man was about to open his mouth to offer some timorous word or two of explanation when all was shrieking and laughter again – the children dancing in a ring, Deg clapping his hands for all he was worth, and Madge whispering into the ear of her mother.

The man closed up his dry mouth and began to attend to the conversation at the head of the bed.

'He is present in this room then, you say, our Madge?' whispered Delphine, though the man could not detect any movement of the lips. Was she some kind of artful ventriloquist then, that daughter of his?

'Have they spoken together? Has he upbraided the man forcefully?'

'No, they have not yet exchanged a single word, mother. In time it must surely happen. Lenny's bark frightened him half out of his skin, and he crept over here into this corner as if half-expecting that we poor women would come to his rescue…'

They pressed their foreheads together and tittered like a pair of naughty infants. The man's face flushed with anger, but, being impatient to hear more, he reined in his tongue.

'And what of the man who took you in and fed you and gave you shelter, our Madge? Is he come yet? Is he in this room? I do not see him…' Madge placed a soothing hand upon her mother's brow, shading the staring eyes.

'Do not trouble yourself with such matters, our mother. He will return in his own good time. He has made his promise, and I know in my heart that he will come again – just as he came that first time.'

'You trust him then, Madge.'

'I do, mother, I do.'

The man felt perplexed by these words, and the desire to interrupt them grew to such a pitch that his mouth opened in spite of itself.

'Who is this man of whom you speak? Is it not the old man who fetched you here? Who is this other man? And when is he coming?'

Madge looked towards him, her face bland, composed, and quite disdainful.

'I did not ask you to chime in with your sillinesses, father. You are my guest in this room, and if you interrupt just once more, I shall tell my brother Deg to throw you out again. No one will lift a finger to help you, so curb your tongue and be patient. Can you not see how sick she is? She must not be troubled by your shrill and pointless gestures. What manner of man are you to behave in this way?'

The man bit his tongue – a little too hard for the good of his own flesh – and fell silent. And though he sighed heavily, he did not remonstrate with her. This was not the moment to match her insolence. He would bide his time.

Then Delphine spoke again. Did she hear our conversation? he asked himself. Does she see me squatting here at the foot of her bed? He raised himself up a little higher. But no, she gave no sign of it. Let her choose to ignore me then, he thought. They are as bad as each other. He would teach them both a lesson in his own good time.

'How is the boy looking then, our Madge? Is he still ruddy of cheek and plump of body? Describe him to me. I hold him so dear, that first-born…'

Such words of affection for one so cussed, thought the man. At the request of her mother, Madge described the boy, telling in the most minute detail imaginable what he had done and seen; whither he had travelled; what he had eaten – whether it be prawn or shrimp or crab; with whom he had spoken – whether it be with farmer, ostler or poacher; what words they had exchanged when they met; what presents he had given to the littlest, and what to the others. And, drawing a tiny purse from her pocket, she opened it up and revealed the contents to her mother behind her hand.

No matter how much he strained, to left or right, up or down, he still could not see what it was that they were discussing with such pride. She will answer for this later, he murmured angrily under his breath.

And so she continued, on and on, with those tales of Deg, and at each new twist and turn of the tale, the mother oohed and aahed – or nodded or frowned or gasped, wide-eyed, or sighed. And he wondered how much longer he could endure such talk. His aching head and paining limbs cried out for a little soothing peace and quiet; his eyelids began to falter shut; he was no longer able to stifle a long, noisy yawn...

When Delphine heard – and saw – that yawn, she snapped at him. 'Have you so little regard for the boy that you cannot bear to hear him spoken of without yawning like an ape? Are you his father or no? Are you not concerned that he left us and has only now returned to the bosom of his family? Were you not aware of his wanderings? Speak to me, man. Have you no words in your mouth?'

He closed his eyes and sought out the words of which she spoke. His fists tightened and tightened, such a tension was building deep inside his body. At last he found the words he thought she wanted. They were afloat on the air, teeming in their thousands, and then whirling and swirling in circles – like a snow storm, he thought. But how could a mere man catch every particle of snow? Was it reasonable to ask him to do so until it had settled and been pounded into a firm whole by human hands?

And that is exactly what he shouted at her, in a voice gruff with indignation: 'Would you ask a mere man to catch the falling snow, woman? Who are you to demand so unseasonable a thing of me? I am nothing more than a husband. I cannot stand the world upon its head. Be contented with words of your own. You shall have mine if and when I choose to give them to you.'

Then, slumping back to the floor, he sulked and frowned and fretted to himself, for he had been sorely agitated by her question.

After pausing to consider his plight for no longer than the blink of an eye, Madge shrugged and turned back to her mother. And, in spite of all his efforts to ignore them, his ears still strained to catch their every word. For what good would it do to forbid the ears to hear? he asked himself reasonably.

'At what hour do you expect him then, our Madge?' asked the mother eagerly.

'He is biding his time – but he will come. And then we shall see what he makes of this creature that is hindering us so.'

Is that me? the man wondered.

'Would you judge him a man of compassion, our Madge?'

'He is kindly – but wholly just. He cannot abide the works of evil.'

The man nodded at those words. We are two

of a kind then, this man and I, he thought.

All of a sudden, Deg spoke up, and at the sound of his voice, all the children fell to the floor, and stared up expectantly into his youthful face.

'Has it a name, that old heap of rags at the foot of our mother's bed?' he asked, pointing across at it. Madge left her mother's side and, walking over to where the man was squatting, she pushed at him with her foot. When he felt the foot strike against his side, he brandished his fist in a gesture of mock-menace, but he soon let it fall again, the better to preserve a little of his manly dignity.

'Do you not know this creature, brother Deg?'

He shook his head. Madge knelt down and whispered into the man's ear: 'Is it not exactly as I foretold? And this is only the beginning…'

'It is meet and right that I should be in this room with my family, and none shall make me budge from this spot,' thundered the man. But when he saw how fierce and cold was the look in his son's eyes, his confidence began to falter. One step at a time now, mister, he advised himself…

Breaking out of that circle of adoring children, the son stepped up to him.

'Tell me what manner of creature you are then – if you can spare me a few of those precious words of yours.'

Stung, the man rose to his feet with a mighty effort, and lurched over his son. He felt giddy on his legs – as if he might at any moment topple over and collapse in a great, humiliated heap. He took his son's arm tenderly – the better to steady himself – and spoke a few imploring words into his ear.

'Do you not own me as your father, Deg? Is this old face of mine–' He pushed it a little closer. '–not familiar to you? Can you not see beneath all the filth and the grime of my everlasting pilgrimage the lineaments of that man who once gave you life?'

Deg scowled up into his face.

'I see nothing but a leering look and a creature that has lost its mind.' At these words the children cheered and Delphine clapped robustly. The man stamped his foot violently upon the floor.

'I shall demonstrate to you all what my words are good for if you continue to insist that you do not know me. Come over here to me, Lenny.'

She rose to her feet and accepted with great reluctance his outstretched hand. He drew her to his side.

'Listen closely, my family, to evidence of the goodness that I have poured into your hearts and minds until those precious cups, such small and delicate vessels, were full to brimming over... Lenny, please repeat over to them the prayer that I taught you.'

'Our Father...' she began, her voice a little faint and husky. But her words were rudely interrupted by that Madge, who shouted out: 'What nonsense is this, old man? You taught her no such words. Was it not God himself who told us these things? And did she not learn them from the Holy Writ? Would you have us believe that you are the author of words that God himself fashioned for our edification? Is it then *you* who are the Almighty God? Is that your real name?'

Delphine clapped her hands again and shrieked with laughter. Deg smirked.

'Must you always behave in this contrary fashion, twisting my words to suit yourself?' the man snapped back at her. 'It was I who taught that Lenny to read. I am her teacher – and yours too. And it was I who gave you breath…'

'No, that school was the place,' piped up Lenny. 'It was there that I learnt God's words from the Tittle-Tattler, our father. Even if we'd listened, there was no good reason to learn because I knew them already…'

'And these children did not proceed from your body, old man,' added Delphine. 'It was God who gave them life and I who bore them. Think a little harder now. Stop up your mouth until you learn to tell the truth!'

'Truth, truth in abundance, is already within,' he exploded. 'What need have I of help? Must I listen to all these lies? ' He looked at each of them in turn, fixing them with his eye. 'If my family will not own me, at least God knows my heart. When He puts me to the test, I will not be found wanting in his eyes, no matter what the miserable judgment of mankind. Do you understand what I say?' He thumped his chest. 'His words are engraved on my heart for all eternity.' He tore open his shirt and jabbed at his rib cage. 'Do you not see them there? Are you all blind?'

No sooner had he said these words than Deg turned on his heel and re-entered the circle, the children took up their dancing again, and Madge resumed the conversation with her mother.

The man gazed wearily upon them all, mumbling to himself, 'I speak and speak – yet still they do not hear. These poor sheep have indeed gone astray. What more can I do for them? I shall sing them all a hymn to sweeten the air.'

He began to hum and to tap his foot in time to the rhythm, and as the humming grew more animated, he took to hopping from foot to foot and turning prettily in a circle. Then he gently clapped his hands. And as he danced and hummed, that circle of children began to break up, and they took up positions on the floor at his feet. Even that Madge knelt down in front of him and gave him the whole of her attention. Delphine alone remained in her corner, staring at the ceiling. How sad that she is so unfeeling, he thought. But it had always been so...

And as he twirled slowly upon his heel, first to the left and then to the right, the door to the room opened and six or seven faces appeared around the door, wary, curious faces seeking his.

'Here I am,' he said, interrupting his own humming in order to beckon them inside, 'make yourselves ready. We are all prepared to receive you.'

When the humming resumed – and the dancing too – the human swarm poured into the room, thick and close-packed as oil, filling all but the smallest space around his feet.

'Do not hold back!' he shouted out to those still beyond the door. 'There is space enough for all in this room.'

And so it seemed, for more and more – and yet more – were entering. Some squatted on their haunches; others lounged against the walls; and still others found a little space on the bed – whether at the foot, up the side, or at the head. The behaviour of these last somewhat surprised him; but when he looked in Delphine's direction, she signalled her assent with a single, broad wink, and this was sufficient to allay his anxieties.

'Bring in that which you faint-hearts have borne upon your heads with such reluctance and trepidation,' he scoffed, but they were clearly not amused that he should have a little fun at their expense.

It was a long time coming. He had counted up twelve complete revolutions of his own body before the end of it rocked unsteadily into view through the door. Now the greatest difficulty was where to lay it down, and they argued long and loud about this matter until the man shouted them down and demanded peremptorily that a space be cleared directly in front of him.

The throng huddled together all the more closely to make a little extra space for the thing. Lenny sat herself down upon Madge's knee and hugged her around the throat. Only Deg still remained standing, sullen and impassive, arms folded in defiance across his chest, with that Dorin clinging to his leg as if to a ship's mast. 'Shortly the boy will see for himself. Have no fear, my heart,' said the man in order to reassure himself.

And so it came on, pitching and tossing across that human sea until it beached at his feet. A great collective sigh went up from the assembled multitude, so relieved were they to be rid of their burden. And still the man mocked their faintheartedness, but this time inside his own head. For now a hush had fallen upon the room in readiness for the ceremony that was to come, and each man stared quietly – if not reverentially – in his direction, though not without the odd suspicious glance from here and there, he thought.

Dorin, who was nestled close to that great box, released his arms from around his brother's leg and, with a whoop of glee, scrambled up its side. Soon he was scurrying back and forth along its narrow top. The crowd buzzed in alarm.

'Push the creature off this minute!' shouted the man, horrified to witness such an act of sacrilege at such a time. Arms reached out for the boy, waving like tendrils, and jerked him off, some pulling at the hair and others at the legs. He screamed as he fell to the floor and began to sob uncontrollably. Deg, with due calm and solemnity, plucked him up from the ground and pressed that sobbing head into his chest.

The man cleared his throat and prepared to speak. Just as he was about to open his mouth to address them, fists hammered upon the door and, without hesitation, it was thrown wide. The old man and the preacher were standing on the threshold, glaring in his direction. He shook a little to see them there.

'Who has given you permission to enter my house?' said Delphine's father.

'But we have had words already,' he stuttered. 'Do you not remember? Can you not see there is important business afoot in this room...'

Still the old man glared. It was like the fixed beam of a torch, that glare of his.

'Indeed, I have seen you – but I did not invite you and your kind to assemble upstairs in this way. Who has given you permission to use my house for this meeting? Answer me that.'

Thinking a cunning thought, the man pointed quickly at Madge, who, having first put Lenny into the arms of a neighbour, stood up to face the newcomer. She was all smiles and sweet talk. It was as if she had known him all her life.

'Don't pay him any mind, grandfather. He thinks he knows everything...'

'He has been sniffing about my house like some dirty mongrel. Is there any privacy that this man will not invade? But is it right for you to encourage him in this ill-mannered behaviour, our Madge?'

See how familiar they are! thought the trapper with contempt. Like two sweets in a jar!

'Should we not give him some rope and see what he does with it?' she replied. The old man smiled at those words.

'Perhaps you do right to disabuse this poor sinner. Hold up your mirror to his wisdom, Madge...'

As they spoke, the trapper's eyes moved from one to the other in utter bewilderment. She has lost me again, he thought.

Then the two of them, the old man and that fat preacher, withdrew quietly. Lenny waved to them as they went, and the disappearing arms returned the gesture. Good riddance say I, murmured the trapper, good riddance to that one and to all his legions...

The Miracle of the Box

Now he had their full attention at last, and his mind and body swelled a little accordingly. 'Before I am most rudely interrupted again, kind people,' he began, scowling down at Madge, but she was not even looking in his direction, 'let me welcome you all to this upstairs room, pilgrims from the furthest corners of the earth...' His arms stretched out as wide as they would go. 'I ask you above all things to attend closely to my words, for today in this room I shall demonstrate, God willing, a miracle that has not been seen since the time our Saviour walked barefoot upon this earth and pronounced it – together with the man and the woman he had fashioned in our own image – holy.' He caught his breath at that word.

'I ask you to turn your attention to the box you bore–' He raised his voice and began to stab his finger into the air above his head. '–with such ill will to this house. I beg of you to search your hearts, beseeching the Lord who is in our midst to forgive you for your unwillingness to bear your share of the burden which, in comparison with the everlasting burden of sin, is light indeed. Bow, bow your heads in shame and implore him to cleanse you, for I have seen with these very eyes–' He pointed now to his eyes. '–and heard with these ears–' He twitched the lobe of an ear. '–how you fought and jostled and argued and complained throughout the execution of this your most sacred duty.'

Eyes blazing, he watched them bow their heads in shame and kiss the plain, unvarnished boards of that room, wailing and pleading forgiveness for their manifold sins. All but the children prostrated themselves in this way. Madge, chin in hand, smiled faintly up at him. She takes me for a ranter, he was thinking to himself.

'And now I ask you — and all you in particular who are seated nearest to our prize — to remove its lid with all speed. Then we shall witness a miracle indeed, and such a one as has not been seen in this benighted hamlet for many a long year...'

Those nearest to him rose eagerly to their feet, and set to work with their bare fists; but soon they gave up, wringing and blowing on their hands in pain, defeated by the many nails which held fast that stout lid. Then one amongst this number, not wholly vanquished, called out for a claw-hammer, and the cry was passed from mouth to ear until it reached one at the back who had been gently dozing. Aroused, and pleased to be pressed into service so unexpectedly, he fished about in his capacious poacher's pockets — the trapper could tell he was a poacher by trade by the mere look on his face — and produced, by and by, that much-desired tool to the manifest pleasure of all those eager lookers on.

It was quickly passed up to the man who had

all this while stood guard, jealous guard, beside the box, flexing his aching fingers; for he was not one to be defeated easily. Taking that great claw-hammer in his fist, he drew those rusted nails forth, one by one, straining at each and every one of them, eleven, twelve and more in all, working his way, with the most painstaking effort, around the perimeter of the box.

And as he worked at his appointed task, the trapper, that orchestrater of miracles to come, sought to distract them with certain words which, to his mind, in that full flush of inner illumination, seemed of great spiritual importance.

'In this room today,' ranted the trapper, 'you will shortly witness a miracle, I say. And it is God's will that this be so. Is it not true that of all things in this world, it is death that we most fear? And who can escape the clutches of death? Name that man!'

He formed his hand into the shape of a crab's claw and made a sudden pinching motion in the air to demonstrate how the pervasive power of death was indeed to be feared by even the most courageous.

'Yet did he not say to us: "fear it not", he asked them with some vehemence, and, "where is its sting?", and, "where is its victory?". It is true, I tell you. That which death has bound, God himself will unloose, whether it be upon this earth or in the hereafter, when we who believe in Him may rejoice together with the heavenly multitude in the high courts of heaven...' He strained up and up on his toes, and directed a single mighty laugh at that ceiling. 'And in order to make all this plain to us, he brought back from the dead one over whom his whole family had wept and moaned. Yes, he called him forth. He renewed his earthly term...'

The man spread out his begrimed palm and gestured graciously, tenderly towards the box. 'See this box we have before us now. Inside, there surely lies the body of some Lazarus – for it is he, Lazarus, of whom I speak; it is he, Lazarus, whom the good Lord restored to life. Now I ask you all to observe with your own eyes what He can do. Prepare yourselves, o my people, to prostrate yourselves in wonderment at his power, for He is indeed in our midst today...'

As he spoke these last words, the man with the claw-hammer removed the thirtieth nail – he told them so himself, with a sweat-soaked grin – and pronounced the job complete. Then, gripping the edges of that lid with his finger ends, he pulled and heaved and prised until his face took on the colour of a ripe summer plum. And, gradually, almost as if unwillingly, it began to rise.

There was a silence in that room of a kind that none had experienced before. Heads strained to see; hands clapped over mouths; even the children, those caterwauling children, seemed frozen in speechless concentration.

When it was part way off, the man stopped and peered inside.

'Is he within?' said the orchestrater of miracles,

impatient that the man should finish the task and throw off the lid without further ado. 'Tell what you are seeing in there, man.'

The kneeling man raised his head. His face was ashen. 'It is stirring all right, mister,' he whispered.

'Fling it off then, man. What are you waiting for?' shouted the trapper.

Suddenly, the lid fell back of its own accord, and the man stepped forth. The onlookers watched in amazement as he began to unwind the bandages from around his body.

'Will he be white and naked beneath those bandages, father?' whispered Lenny.

'Of course not, Lenny,' snapped the trapper. 'He died in his night shirt, which they did not take off him. That was the custom.'

The crowd was so astonished that they kissed the dead man and hugged him, and the children played with the bandages as if it were the Mayday Festival.

'Jesus helps everybody, he is everybody's friend,' the trapper shouted. 'He is ready to do his miracles any time we ask him.'

Jamie looked up. 'But where is this Jesus, father, to do these things? How can he do them if he is not here?'

'I am coming to that, Jamie. Be a little patient now, boy.'

FINIS

Epilogue

It is a tale of reason drowned in phantasmagoria, this account of the inner and outer worlds of Joseph Tredinnick, rabbit trapper by trade, late of Porthcothan Bay, Cornwall. And it is based on stories told to the author by Tredinnick's bachelor friend and near neighbour, Harold Tresco (it was Tresco who owned the caravan in which Tredinnick lived for the greater part of his free life), a farmer and Sunday painter of sorts who eked out a modest living on some sixty odd acres, little more than half a mile up the valley from Porthcothan Bay as the crow flies.

After Tredinnick had confessed to the murders of Delphine Trethewy (his common-law wife) and Thomas ('Ginger') Trethewy, a farm labourer of Newlyn East, he was committed to Bodmin Jail for the duration of his natural life, the twin charges of murder having been commuted to manslaughter on the grounds of diminished responsibility.

After five years and seven months of incarceration, Rosie Pentreath, one of the Sisters of Charity who resided in the convent at St Mawgan-in-Pydar, some three miles from the spot where Tredinnick had lived, hearing one day from a friend the tragic tale of his delusions and their sorry outcome, took pity on the man and asked to visit him in his cell. It was the first visitor he had had for two years, four months and three days, he told her,

Harold Tresco being too crippled up with the arthritis to make the arduous journey any longer.

This most merciful sister sought and gained permission from all the authorities concerned, both spiritual and temporal, that ruled over her, to take Tredinnick back to St Mawgan, and there he spent the last years of his life, fasting and praying that God might forgive him for his misdeeds.

Every Thursday, he was allowed to spend an hour or two, weather permitting, walking around the sequestered kitchen garden of the Convent, inspecting the flowers and the vegetables that grew there in such profusion. He was a man with a good eye for a leek, though there was, to my knowledge, not one iota of Welsh blood in him.

On the Thursday of his disappearance, the weather was most changeable, and that, according to the Sister, may have precipitated his sudden change of mood. In spite of the fact that it would surely be deemed a most uncommon feat for an ailing man of seventy-three to scale a perimeter wall of some six and one half feet in height, Tredinnick managed it somehow. His body was found on the morning of the next day – Good Friday as it happens – floating face down in the rock pool at the northernmost tip of Porthcothan Bay, the very place where, he insisted to his death, he had drowned his son Deg.

No matter how many times Deg insisted, in those weekly letters to his father (the boy emigrated to Australia at the age of twenty-four and never clapped eyes on his parent again) that he was far from dead, the father never saw fit to reply to a single one of them.

'That boy is a wraith — and a mischievous one at that!' he would say to old Harold Tresco when the latter commented, as he so often did, upon the great heap of unopened letters on his prison table, whistling at the sight of so much mail from far-flung places, Tresco himself having never gone further than Exeter in his life. But would Tredinnick let him have just a few of those colourful stamps for a favourite nephew?

'Let them lie,' was all the old trapper ever said, and so, by and by, Tresco stopped bothering.

Acknowledgements

Multiple thanks for permission to reproduce "Adrift," the painting on the jacket of this book: to its artist, Ruth Dupré, its owners, Ian Hargreaves and Adele Blakebrough, and its photographer, Joe Andrews.

About the author

Michael Glover is a Sheffield-born, Cambridge-educated, London-based poet and art critic, and Poetry Editor of *The Tablet*. He writes weekly for *Hyperallergic Weekend*, and has written regularly for the *Independent*, *The Times*, the *Financial Times*, the *New Statesman* and *The Economist*. He has also been a London correspondent for *ARTNews*, New York. His recent books include: *Late Days* (2018), *Hypothetical May Morning* (2018), *Neo Rauch* (2019), *The Book of Extremities* (2019), *What You Do With Days* (2019) *John Ruskin: a dictionary* (2019), *Thrust: a spasmodic history of the cod-piece in art* (2019) and *Rose Wylie* (2020). Last year he also published *Whose?*, a dramatic monologue, and *One Season In Hell (Une Saison en Enfer)*, a version of a classic of 19th century French literature by Arthur Rimbaud, both with 1889books.

Message from 1889 books, Sheffield independent publisher

If you enjoyed reading *The Trapper*, I'd really appreciate a review on Amazon, Goodreads or whatever book review sites you use: just a line or two would be great. Reviews and personal recommendations are really appreciated by authors and will help an independent publisher such as *1889 Books* grow stronger.

Steven Kay, publisher